The Scent of Apples

The Scent of Apples

STORIES BY

OLIVIA DAVIS

BOSTON

HOUGHTON MIFFLIN COMPANY

1972

Some of these stories were originally published in *Four
Quarters*, *The Kenyon Review*, *The Malahat Review*, *Prairie Schooner*,
Queen's Quarterly, and *The Virginia Quarterly Review*.

First Printing   v

For Sebastian, Miranda,
and Penelope

Table of Contents

The Scent of Apples

Loss and Chaos

AFTER THE TRAIN JOURNEY there was the ship. To William, only confusion lay in between, though later he was to remember vaguely the enormous piles of luggage in the customs shed, a hundred times taller than himself, and the white faces of strangers looming all around him. He knew, of course, that they were going aboard a ship, and expected it to be riding splendidly at anchor somewhere where he could really see it. He thought he could smell the sea, and looked about hopefully, pictures in his mind of sand and shells, buckets and spades, but he couldn't see through or around all the trousered legs and fur coats surrounding him. Hanging on tightly to his mother's hand, he was swept along passages and corridors, up and down, and the smell of the sea was overcome by the smell of fresh paint and varnish. At the end of all the passages was a quiet white room that William's mother called "our cabin." She had told him the story of Robinson Crusoe, who had built himself a cabin and had a goat, but this was not a bit like what William had imagined. It was just another, an ordinary, room. His mother took her hat off, and tossed it on one of the beds.

"Well, we're on our way at last," she said. "Good-bye, New York!"

"Are we on the ship now?" asked William, wondering how it had come about, sure it couldn't be so.

"I just said so," said his mother. She loosened her fur coat, letting it slip down a little from her shoulders, and checked the luggage which stood neatly in the middle of the cabin floor. William was delighted to recognize the suitcases he hadn't seen for so long, and patted one of them with his hand.

"Don't stand there mooning like that, William," she said. "Take your coat off." While he struggled with his buttons, she opened one of the suitcases, and got out his pajamas and handed them to him. She pulled drawers open and pushed them shut, and put things away, and when she turned back to him he was still standing there quietly with his coat half-unbuttoned and his pajamas in his hand.

"What are you waiting for?" she said.

"My duck," said William. His blue and white stuffed duck that he had taken to bed with him for as long as he could remember.

"You left it on the train," said his mother. "You won't miss it. You're too big for stuffed toys, and anyway you were allergic to it. I only let you keep it because . . . well . . ." She moved her shoulders irritably, leaving the sentence unfinished, and William cast his eyes down while he went on with the task of undressing. He didn't really believe he had left it on the train. His mother had sometimes said that, if she saw him trailing that wretched thing around just one more time, she'd throw it away. He couldn't imagine the duck lying alone on the prickly plush seat that had scratched the backs of his knees. The duck belonged where it usually was, under his left arm. Only a really painful desire to have it with him had brought him to mention it, and he knew he would never speak of it again.

"Daddy wouldn't like to see you crying about an old stuffed toy," she said warningly. William was an expert at holding his eyelids so wide that tears wouldn't fall out, and he did so now. He couldn't remember much about Daddy; he was gone for so long and so often. But his feelings of sadness and inhibition were reinforced. He thought of unhappy meal-times, of food congealing on his plate, of the atmosphere about him always charged, the air too heavy for him to breathe. He didn't like what he felt, and something — perhaps those preternaturally wide eyes — gave him away, for his mother told him sharply to get right into bed. At once, this minute.

He was a slow-moving child, and the more people cracked commands at him the slower he went, but he climbed into bed obediently enough, and laid his head back on the pillow, his eyes on his mother. Something made her relent, for she brought the pillow from her own bed and put it under the one he already had, so that he was lying in his usual position, half sitting up.

"The steward can bring me more pillows," she said, brushing her hand quickly across William's hair. "I don't want you getting sick. You must remember you're a big boy now, going away on a long trip." It was nice, her touching his hair like that, and he was pretty sure he wouldn't be sick. He was going away, going on a long trip, like people did, like people were always doing. His mother had been on long trips, stooping quickly to kiss William good-bye, and then gone for timeless periods, while the blossoms paled and fell from the trees, the leaves grew bigger, and the fruit swelled. His father was always gone. He was gone, in a sense, even when he was there, before he got up from the dinner table and shut himself in his study. "You must do what's best, Myra." He was gone when his briefcase stood in the hall, covered with tickets and labels. "I'll be back soon. Take care of that asthma of yours." As though the asthma were a companion, like the blue and white duck.

Even William's best friend, down the street, with whom he had tricycled forever, had gone away. "The Cadillac of tricycles," said his father, with a little, sarcastic snort. "I got the best I could find. But I don't much like that child he's chosen to play with."

"Mrs. Wrysinski watches them," said his mother. "Anyway, the family's leaving soon. Going to California, I think." But the long summer had come and gone, and his mother and father had set off on trips here and there as they always did, and Joey Boy was still around, his legs pumping furiously next to William's when they had tricycle races down the street together. In the fall, Joey announced casually that he was leaving the next day.

"We're going to California," he said, and shot William in the knee with his imaginary six-shooter. That night, William was quite ill, and Mrs. Wrysinski, the housekeeper, had to send for the doctor, since both his mother and his father were away. He was in bed when the moving van came, and when Joey Boy and his mother arrived to say good-bye.

"Maybe it's the heat," said Mrs. Wrysinski. "Though, the Lord knows, he's allergic to *everything*."

"I don't know. They say it's a nervous thing," said Joey's mother.

"See you," said Joey Boy airily.

"See you," gasped out William. But he knew he wouldn't.

And now he too was going away, leaving people behind, like Mrs. Wrysinski, who would be sad because he was gone.

"I won't get sick," he promised his mother, and at that moment the door to the cabin burst open, and a man with a fair mustache came in, with bags in each hand.

"Oops, sorry! Wrong cabin," he said immediately. He caught sight of William. "Sorry, kid," he said. "Wouldn't have disturbed the sleeping prince for worlds."

"He's not asleep," said William's mother, smiling. "It's all right."

"Mr. Rowley," called someone behind the man, someone in a white jacket. "Mr. Rowley, you're next door, sir."

"See you on deck," said the man, puffing through his mustache in what William thought was an extremely amusing manner, and vanished.

"All right," said his mother. "Go to sleep. I may go out on deck for a while, later on." She sat down at the dressing table, and slipped her fur coat altogether off. William's last memory of her that night was of her leaning forward and making an O of her mouth as she applied lipstick.

·

In the morning, he opened his eyes to find the room behaving strangely, lifting up and coming back down again. Everything creaked, and his red and white robe swung on its hook. For a moment, William was alarmed, and felt about for his duck, but then he remembered where he was, and sat up in bed. He was on a ship, and it was moving. His mother, in the other bed, was still asleep, and he went across to waken her. Leaning over, he changed his mind, and climbed onto the bed beside her. He hadn't often seen her asleep, for she didn't like his coming into her room. She was always busy dressing or doing her face, and it was a long time since he had stood in her doorway in the early morning, the stuffed duck under one arm and a blanket trailing from his hand. He put his face close to hers on the pillow, and thought what a lot of cigarettes she smoked, smelling them on her breath and seeing the ashtray on the night stand almost full. She opened her eyes and looked at him blankly. He thought she didn't know who he was, and he almost told her, "It's me, it's William," but then she really woke up, shaking the sleep out of her.

"Oh, it's you," she said.

"The ship's moving."

"We sailed at midnight. Go and get dressed."

.

After breakfast, there was the sea, double doors pushed open against the wind on deck, a glimpse of gray and white water, a staircase with an iron railing they had to hold on to tightly, and William's mother telling him to stay in the ship's play-room while she walked with the fair-mustached stranger who had burst into their cabin the night before.

The playroom was furnished with big yellow and scarlet blocks. A great many children were there already, more than William was used to seeing in one place. Somehow, although it was the first day out for all of them, the other children seemed more familiar with the place than William was, to have taken it over already as their own, to regard him, who had arrived perhaps five minutes later than they themselves, as the only real stranger in the room. He stood it as long as he could, leaning against the enormous windows, where he could see a little bit of the deck, waiting for his mother and her companion to come around again, and resisting the efforts of the woman in charge of the playroom to draw him into the games. He slipped out while the woman was serving juice and crackers from a cart. He climbed down the iron staircase and went running, lolloping lolloping, along the deck. He had it in mind to get to the end, the very end, of the ship, where the seagulls flew in a wreath over the waves, when he heard his mother cry out.

"*There* he is! William, stop!" And of course he was caught, expertly, in the arms of the stranger.

"How did you get out of the playroom?" asked his mother.

"I ran out."

"Smart kid," said the man. "I wouldn't want to be shut up in there myself." They laughed, and William thought maybe they were laughing at him, and clutched a fistful of his mother's skirt. "No, I mean it," said the man. "He ought to be out on deck; get some color in his cheeks." He bent down and looked at William. "I'm Rowley," he said. "Think you can remember that?"

"Like the frog?" said William.

The man looked puzzled, and William's mother explained. "It's a song he knows," she said. "Heigho, says Rowley. A frog he would a-wooing go."

"Oh, sure," said Rowley. He was looking at William's

mother, and William was aware of the impact of eyes, as hard as a blow, laden with secrets that had nothing to do with him.

"And my mother," said William. "Do I call her Mistress Mouse?" He felt more confident now, for something about Rowley reminded him of a frog. The mustache — was it? — that made the mouth look wider than it was. The round blue eyes? The greenish tweed suit, flecked with brown?

"Why not?" said Rowley. "We'll both call her Mistress Mouse."

His mother laughed, and gave a mock curtsy, and the boy thought he had been the cause of it. He smiled, too, and stood looking at them both, pleased because something had been settled. Someone near them gave an exclamation, and people rushed to the ship's rail.

"Porpoises! A school of porpoises!"

Rowley lifted him up. "There, over there; do you see them?"

William looked straight down where the water threshed away from the side of the ship, and then away to the tilting horizon. He was about to shake his head, for he hadn't seen anything, but his mother caught his arm.

"Look at them," she said. "They're beautiful, and playing just like children." She wanted him to see them, so William nodded and, after a moment, Rowley put him down and straightened his jacket for him.

"This is the life," he said to William. "A life on the ocean wave, hey?" A steward walked by, solemnly tapping a little gong with a stick. People drifted away from the rail. The porpoises were gone. "Time for lunch, Mistress Mouse," said Rowley. "Why don't I change tables and join you two?

Or would this gentleman object?" He stood between them and placed one hand on William's head.

"Don't be ridiculous," said William's mother, laughing. "Do join us."

They went down together, and William sat opposite them at the table, sorry because he hadn't seen the porpoises and couldn't ask what they were without revealing that he hadn't seen them; glad because they were all sitting together and being gay and funny with one another. Rowley was nice and cheerful and made his mother smile, and together they smiled at William.

"He's too thin," said Rowley. "You ought to make him eat more." It was quite different from the way his father said it.

"I try," his mother said to Rowley, "but he never has any appetite. He's delicate. Nervy." She moved her shoulders a little, as though to cast off an unwanted thought.

"Sea air must be agreeing with him, though," said Rowley. "Look at him now. I don't know where he's putting it. A few more days on this ship and he'll have an obesity problem. The food must be better, hey, boy?"

William grinned shyly through a ring of tomato soup, and helped himself clumsily to great spoonfuls of vegetables to go with the meat on his plate. It wasn't that the food was nicer, it was that the air was thinner, people were smiling, he could breathe.

"The porpoises were playing with a little red ball," he volunteered, as finally they sat silent over coffee. A minute tide was visible in the cups, reminding him that they were on a ship. He imagined infinitesimal seagulls, flying over the moving liquid.

"William!" mocked his mother, but kindly. "I don't believe you saw them at all."

"Why, Mistress Mouse! He certainly did," said Rowley.
"They were playing with a red ball. I saw it, too."

"And singing, too, no doubt," said his mother.

"Maybe," said Rowley. "My hearing isn't so good. I missed
that."

William relaxed into a vision of the porpoises as they must
have been. White armed, golden haired, singing, and playing
with a red ball. He wished he really had seen them.

.

He didn't have to go back to the playroom again. The days
passed delightfully in the company of Rowley and his mother.
Sometimes, they sat on long chairs in the sun, and Rowley
wrapped him in a blanket so that only his eyes and the tip of
his nose showed. Sometimes he was unwrapped, with boister-
ous suddenness.

"Time for a walk, Billy boy," said Rowley. "Time to check
up on the captain." Or, "How about a drink? Your mother
can come along if she wants to" (winking furiously). And
off they all went to the bar.

William grew used to following Rowley's tweedy legs along
the deck, up the iron staircases, on a tour of the bridge one
afternoon, when Rowley explained exactly how the ship
worked.

"Going to be a great engineer, this kid," said Rowley when
they came down again. "Understood every word. Mechanical
genius." His father had thought otherwise. "He can't understand the simplest things," said his father. "I tried to show

him in the car today. He just shut up like a clam." And now, too, he shut up like a clam. He hadn't in fact understood much, but not for anything would he have disappointed Rowley, so he nodded, round eyed, at his mother.

In the bar, he was given a drink of his own, a Coke, embellished with a slice of orange and a cherry.

"Happy landings!" said Rowley, and William became intoxicated by association, watching his mother and Rowley sip something pale, watching their faces become bland and gentle, their eyes all-seeing yet unseeing, his mother's hand raised tenderly to restore the slightest of order to her prettily blown hair. When it was time for him to go to his own early dinner, he was gay and giggly, and Rowley shushed him on the stairs and in the elevator.

At night, his mother took him to their cabin and put him to bed. She was kinder, gentler than he had ever known her, helping him with his pajamas, telling him stories. While he lay in bed and watched, she dressed beautifully for the grown-up dinner that came later, and left him with a kiss and a quick brush of her fingers over his hair when Rowley knocked on the door.

"Coming, Mistress Mouse?" said Rowley, and, sticking his head inside the door, "Good night, Billy boy. Sleep tight!"

William snuggled down in the blankets that were becoming familiar, and slept. At intervals, he woke again, and listened to the sound of the air conditioner, and the deep, muffled noise of the ship's engines, and wondered when his mother would come back. One night, he got out of bed and opened the cabin door to look along the passage. The stewardess saw him, and sent him inside again. He let her tuck him in without protest. Beyond her hurrying figure, he had seen his mother and Rowley going into Rowley's cabin and closing the door behind them. Satisfied, because he knew where his mother was, he went to sleep.

.

Once they got there, the mysterious *there* to which the ship was proceeding, William supposed he would see his father, but there was another train ride, and a hotel where his mother explained that it would be some time before they saw Daddy. She was staying in Paris, she said, to shop. Rowley was in Paris, too — on business, he said.

For a while, everything was as it had been. They went up on the roof of an enormous church, and Rowley showed William ugly little creatures carved out of stone, leaning out and grinning down at the people below. While his mother and Rowley were kissing each other, William leaned so far over the parapet that his mother screamed. Rowley grabbed the back of his jacket, and held on so tight he thought he would choke.

"Don't worry, Myra, I've got him," said Rowley. He gave William a little shake. "What are you trying to do? Turn us gray?" he said.

Afterward, they had hot chocolate and a plate of little cakes in a restaurant. It seemed to William that it was about then that things began to change. Rowley was as nice and funny as ever, but his mother seemed to argue a lot, and Rowley stopped calling her Mistress Mouse. On one day, they went to a place they called The Bois, and William, with a lance in his hand, rode a wooden horse and tried to spear brass rings as the carousel took him around. It was late in the year, and cold, and there were no other children around. When he came to the place where Rowley and his mother were standing, he waved the lance in the air; but they weren't really looking at him, they were talking to each other; and he missed the ring every time he went by. Rowley bought him a balloon, and William had a sudden image of his mother as a beautiful balloon like this one, violet colored, vibrant, filled not with air but with some magic substance, tugging to get away. His mother told him to wind the string around his wrist, but it was like a bird; it wanted to fly; and it was half on purpose — unwillingly, but half on purpose — that he let it slip through his fingers. She got mad about it. It was a present from Rowley; he had only had it five minutes. It was the same every time — give him something and he lost or broke it. Even Rowley seemed disappointed in him. They watched the purple globe, swaying gently, caught in the trees above them. It hadn't got very far. William thought he might as well have kept it, after all.

"We'll get another," said Rowley, but the balloon man had gone.

In the hotel lobby, William's mother and Rowley talked for a long time while William clung to his mother's skirt and looked up at them both. He remembered when all conversations had been like this, had all excluded him, had all made the air heavy and difficult to breathe. Rowley, William thought, wanted them to stay in Paris, or go somewhere else with him. His mother said be sensible. She said they had had a lot of fun, but Rowley was spoiling it, making it all too difficult, too complicated. Let's not run it into the ground, she said.

At last, and it was last night she had said it, she announced, "We go tomorrow. I've called Cook's to fix up the tickets."

His father, William understood, was in Rome. They were on their way to join him. Now they were really on their way. The luggage was packed and ready to be taken away. William stood in the middle of the rug while his mother tied his shoe-laces for him. The hotel room was empty and impersonal. His mother's things were gone from the dressing table; William's robe and pajamas were packed. He hadn't anything else, and for a moment he remembered his blue and white duck and felt sad and melancholy, wanting something of his own to hold in his hand.

"Tomorrow you will see Daddy," said his mother, but William was concentrating on his breathing, and had no responses to give her.

"Don't you want to see Daddy?" she asked him.

He examined her face for the answer, but couldn't find it in that pretty, brittle, carefully enameled mask. Nevertheless, he knew she wanted something from him. To answer a need with an affirmative was more natural with him now than it had been before the trip, and he nodded. "Yes, I do," he said. "I do want to see Daddy."

She puzzled him further by turning away and sighing, fiddling indecisively with the straps of the luggage. "So do I," she said. "I'll be glad when we get there, when it's all over."

William supposed she meant the journey, on which he seemed to have been moving all his life. He understood, too, that there was some hurry, but they waited for a long time in the hotel room until the men came to take away the suitcases. Another man, in uniform and with a band on his hat, arrived, and gave William's mother an envelope, and told her something about changing trains.

"Is he a French soldier?" asked William. The man smiled and looked at his mother, and for a moment everything was sweet and golden again. He had said the right thing; he had struck the right note.

"So, you know what a soldier is?" He gave a kind, grownup smile to William's mother, and left, patting William on the head.

"*Is* he a soldier?" said William, wanting to know, wanting to repeat his triumph.

"Of course not. He's the man from Cook's," said his mother, and glanced at her wrist watch. "It's time to go."

They went down in the little golden cage that was the elevator, where William always felt holy, as though he were in church, as though silence and stiffness were the proper thing, and going up and down a ceremonial, and then they went outside the hotel, where there were chairs and tables in the weak morning sunshine, and little trees in white-painted tubs. It would be winter soon. The trees were almost bare, and the wind was cold. A taxi had been ordered and was already waiting, but just as they were about to climb in William's mother paused.

"Here he comes," she said, with such mockery and amusement in her voice that William turned, expecting to see — what? A troupe of clowns, an elephant, a cageful of monkeys, perhaps. But it was Rowley, rocking toward them in his greenish tweed suit, puffing through his mustache, his blue eyes wider and rounder than ever. William ran to him and embraced his legs, too pleased to speak.

"Hi, there, Billy boy," said Rowley. "My dear Myra!"

"This wasn't wise," said William's mother. "Not wise at all."

William found his voice. "You're coming with us," he said.

"Well, no. Just to the station," said Rowley. "Thought I'd come and see you off."

They went in the taxi to the station. The train for Italy was already in. Rowley bought William's mother a bundle of American magazines, and a little model of the Eiffel Tower.

"Put it in your handbag," he said. "It's to remember me by."

William thought a model of a ship would have been better, but he said nothing, only clung to his mother as people hurried past, talking to each other in French, and the porters shouted. Puffs of steam were coming out between the wheels of the train. Someone banged the corner of a suitcase against William's legs, and he began to cry, not so much from the pain of the blow as from frustration, that the general sense of urgency and important haste had not communicated itself to his mother. He wanted to board the train. Even though it would be uncomfortable — he remembered the other train, the plush seats scratching the backs of his legs, and his lost duck — even though he knew Rowley was staying behind, he wanted to board the train. Until they did so, until they found their seats and sat down in them, this final stage of their journey could not begin.

"Hey, don't do that," said Rowley. "We can't have every-body crying. I'll start myself, in a minute. Here, I've got something for you." He handed William a little box with a cellophane lid, tied with gold string. Inside were two candy animals, a frog and a mouse. "Good-bye, old Billy boy," he said, touching William's cheek with the back of his hand. "It's been nice knowing you. Don't forget me. It's time," he went on. "You'd better get in."

William was lifted up the steep steps, and turned to see his mother and Rowley with their arms about each other. The train began, very gently, to move, and William gave an alarmed cry. Rowley helped her onto the step. She waved once, and then ushered the boy before her down the corridor, as the train slid out of the station.

"Will we see him again?" said William. "Will he come to Rome?"

"I don't suppose so," said his mother. She seemed quite composed as she found their seats and smiled at the man sitting opposite. "Don't look so glum," she told William, in the voice she reserved for use when other people were present, full of a mocking raillery. "Tomorrow you'll be seeing Daddy." She helped him off with his coat, and sat down and opened a magazine, while the man opposite looked at her interestedly.

William stared out of the window for a long time, his lip trembling as he considered all he was leaving behind. Kind Rowley, waving good-bye. His blue and white duck, left on a long-ago train. Then he turned his attention to the box Rowley had given him, and took out the frog. It was wonderfully tinted, and looked exactly like a frog — greenish with flecks of brown, the underneath a yellowy orange. It was made of almond paste. William clutched it tightly in his hand. He would keep it forever. He would never eat it.

"You American?" said the man opposite. "I knew you were. You just had to be. How about a drink before lunch? The restaurant car's just about one car down."

William's mother was smiling, lifting one hand to adjust

her hat. "I'd love to," she said. "William, will you be all right here?"

He nodded, and they got up and went out, sliding the compartment door closed behind them. William thought about how he would keep the frog, how he would put it back in the box with the cellophane lid, so that he could always look at it when he wanted to, and it would always remind him of Rowley. After a while, he realized with shame and horror that he had been nibbling at the frog all the time he was thinking about it, and it was already half-eaten. Filled with a strange despair, he ate the rest in two large bites, and hunted for the crumbs on his shirt and trousers. He still had the mouse. He would keep that. He looked at it, amazingly life-like, with little whiskers made of string, tiny black eyes, two small white teeth showing in front. But he felt sick. He had eaten too much, and he shouldn't have eaten at all. After a long struggle, he got the top of the window open, and threw away the box, with the mouse still in it.

When his mother came back with the man who shared their compartment, she found William asleep. His breathing was labored and difficult. Around his mouth was a sticky, sugary rim, and when she bent over him she could smell almonds. Years later, as she bent over William for the last time, the last person who ever would bend over him, she smelled them again. But then they were bitter, the very heart and core of his trouble.

The Other Child

I saw the whole thing. I didn't snoop. I didn't have to. They carried on, day after day, right there on the open beach, immediately under our noses. Or at least under mine, since a nose without a pair of eyes above it isn't much good, and Lansing is blind.

We'd sit out most of the day on the porch of the little cottage I'd rented for the summer, Lansing slumped in his chair, hands folded across his stomach. You never knew if he was asleep or not. I'd read, or sew, and there would be the three of them, the young woman and her little boy and the lifeguard, sitting practically under the porch railings, so we could hear every word they said.

I guess that as far as they were concerned, Lansing and I were invisible, simply not there, two stuffy old people sitting on a porch. They probably thought, if they gave us any thought at all, that we were husband and wife, rather than mother and son. Other people have thought that. Lansing has gone to seed in the past years, mostly through lack of exercise I suppose, and he's very bald for a man of thirty-five. There's a look-alike quality about us, the kind of look that descends on husbands and wives when they've been married for a great many years. Oddly, it amuses me to augment this. I wear seersucker suits, and white blouses, and I bought a couple of straw hats the first day we came, and made Lansing wear one while I wore the other.

So there we sat, two people of indeterminate age, and scarcely determinable sex, in cone-shaped white straw hats, summer suits and dark glasses, while a few yards away the young woman in the yellow bathing suit played with her baby in the sand. Sometimes, when he had fallen asleep in the shade of the striped umbrella, she sat and wrote long letters on blue paper, which as often as not she tore up afterward, stuffing the pieces in the big beach bag she had. Then she would pull her knees up under her chin and stare out to sea. Sometimes she looked as though she might be crying. I had her sized up pretty well. I knew what would happen, and I was right. The lifeguard stand was off to the left, just a short way away, with a little white rowboat tied to its base, so if it were needed the lifeguard would have to push it only a foot or two into the water. There were two lifeguards for this stretch of beach, working in shifts, and the young woman spent no more than a couple of days looking lonely and pathetic before one of them noticed her, and came over to talk to her, and play with the baby. It wasn't five minutes before he was sitting on the blanket with her, and after about ten minutes they were calling each other Johnny and Rose as though they'd known each other all their lives. It turned out that the little boy's name was Johnny, too.

"What a coincidence," said the lifeguard. The baby was called after his father, she told him. He was in New York,

No, he wouldn't be joining them. She was divorced. It was all quite recent, just a week or two ago. She had come away with the baby to sort things out, decide what to do next.

"Gee," said the lifeguard. I suppose his expression could be called typically youthful, earnest, sincere, sympathetic — you see, I know all the words — but to me it was stupid. I laughed. Nature, playing her fool tricks. It always amuses me. You'd think people would be more alert, would notice themselves more, but I've lived long enough to find out they aren't, and they don't. Anyway, I made some sort of small noise, and Lansing turned his dark-glassed face to me.

"They sound nice," he said. "What do they look like?"

Sometimes I don't answer Lansing, when he asks me this about people. You wouldn't understand it, if you hadn't lived, year in, year out, with a blind person, as I have. I get a strange feeling, sometimes, not telling him. But this time I did.

"Nice? I doubt it. That yellow suit she has on is hardly decent. Her hair's bleached. I can see the roots growing out. The young fellow, the lifeguard? He's one of those college boys, working for the summer. You can't tell one from the other, they're all as alike as peas in a pod, they all need haircuts. Nice? She came down to the beach to pick up a man, and he's it. What's nice about that?"

"There's a baby, isn't there?" said Lansing. "Doesn't that make it more — pleasant?" This time, I was silent. Lansing kept his head turned toward me for a moment, a peculiar twist to his mouth, and then he turned away.

"Maybe they'll get married, and live happily ever after," he said.

On the beach, the girl called Rose got up, and took long-legged strides after the baby, who had wandered a little distance away. She carried him back, and set him down on the blanket.

"Naughty Johnny," she said. "You stay right here." She hugged him. "I have to watch him every minute," she told the lifeguard. "He's at that age. And all boy. He can hardly walk yet, but if I just turn my back for a second, wowee!"

"You see," said Lansing, "she likes her baby."

"I'll watch him for you, if you want to go and swim," said the lifeguard. She declined, giggled, finally accepted, pulled on a white rubber bathing cap, and ran down to the water.

"The young fellow, big Johnny, he likes the baby too," said Lansing.

"Why not?" I asked sharply. "He's a perfectly ordinary child. Nothing wrong with him." Lansing sighed.

"Perfectly ordinary, yes. So I gathered." I got up.

"I'll make some lemonade." In the kitchen, I wondered if Lansing had been needling me. There had been that sardonic look on his face, but it is always hard to know what Lansing is thinking, or if he thinks about anything at all. Mostly he seems a great blind vegetable, merely existing. But then again, he can come out with a remark that shows he is sharp enough. *Perfectly ordinary.* To be ordinary is to be perfect, as Lansing knows. I took two glasses of lemonade out to the porch, but Lansing didn't answer me when I spoke, or take the glass I touched against his hand. He had apparently fallen asleep. I sat down with my embroidery. The lifeguard was climbing the ladder to his chair, and the girl and the child were building a sand castle. There should be peace for an hour or so, I thought, unless the child should start to cry.

I watched him, playing with his mother in the sand, a perfectly formed male child, no blemish, no scar, no deformity. At that age, eighteen months, two years old perhaps, Lansing had been tied to a tree at the end of a long rope, his area of freedom perhaps twelve feet in diameter, carefully cleared of everything that could possibly hurt him. Not that he had any disposition to wander. He was timid, frightened, dependent, his forehead covered with bruises. Years of bitterness rose in my throat. Harold had left me, in spite of our child having been born blind. He gave me money, he took nothing with him, but he said he couldn't stand it any longer, what he called my possessiveness, my tricks. I can't take it any longer, Nettie, Harold said. Find someone stronger than I am, someone who's up to it. But of course I hadn't. This girl on the beach, this Rose, she was younger than I had been, she would find someone. This Rose, and her healthy baby. Lansing had been born to me late. I really hadn't ever expected to marry, much less have a child. He had been born blind, and the child on the beach could see.

"Are they leaving?" said Lansing. The soft chatter of the mother and child had awakened him. They were gathering their things together; she was trying to make him do his share of the work, sending him in search of his toys, his bucket and spade, a red ball. "There it is," she said. "Go and get it, Johnny. See it?" See it, see it, see it. She folded the blanket, and they walked up the beach, pausing beneath the lifeguard's stand to say something, too far away to hear. They climbed the low sand dunes, and disappeared. This was their third day. Later she would come back alone, for an hour or two in the early evening.

"Yes," I said. "They've gone."

"Quiet, without them," said Lansing, after a moment. "There don't seem to be many people about." He sounded less neutral, more melancholy than usual.

"I chose it for that," I reminded him. "You don't care for crowds of people."

"Of course," said Lansing politely. "You were perfectly right."

"We could go for a stroll after supper," I suggested. Lansing turned his heavy, pasty face from side to side. He had never seen a quick, negative shake of the head. All his movements were slow and deliberate.

"No, no. I'd rather not. But perhaps you'd like to go for a walk, by yourself?"

"And leave you alone? Certainly not. We'll have an early supper, and play chess afterward."

.

While I was in the kitchen, preparing the trays, the girl Rose came back to the beach. She sat in the same place as before, the way people do, and the lifeguard, off duty now, joined her. They were talking as loudly as ever, totally unaware, or uncaring of us, as I silently placed Lansing's tray on his knees, and sat down with my own.

"They're back," said Lansing. "Is she still wearing the hardly decent bathing suit?" She had changed into a light blue cotton dress. She was deeply tanned.

"Yes, she's still wearing it," I said. "She got a burn this afternoon. She ought to put something on it." Lansing was silent for a moment, considering.

"It's got cooler," he said. "She'll catch cold."

"More fool her."

"Rose, you have the strangest eyes," said the lifeguard. "Sort of green."

"They are not!" She laughed, a foolish, come-hither kind of laugh.

"They are too." The sort of thing that could go on all night.

"They're the same color as this. See?" She held up a fold of her skirt to her face.

"Yeah. I guess you're right. But sometimes they do look green."

"Well, they're not. Blue. True blue, Dad used to say."

"Where's my stick, Mother?" asked Lansing. A sudden panic seemed to have struck him. I watched him. Then, "Right beside your chair, Lansing. Why? Where did you think it was?" With it in his hand, the panic seemed assuaged. He reached out with it, touched the porch railings, rattled them gently.

"I don't know," he said lightly. "I thought I might have lost it, like I did before." I wondered if he knew I had hidden it, that time. I don't know what made me do it. And I didn't really hide it, merely moved it from the side of the chair where he always put it, to the other side. Everything always had to be in exactly the same place, for Lansing. I didn't let him grope for long, just a minute or two, and then I handed the stick to him. Perhaps it was the extravagance of his relief that made me feel rewarded.

"Honest," said the lifeguard. "He's the cutest kid I ever saw."

"When did you ever learn to be an expert with kids?" said the girl Rose.

"Got five brothers and sisters," said the lifeguard, and told her all their names. "And I was lifeguard at a summer camp last year. *And* taking sociology at school. I'd like to find something to do, in that way, you know."

"I bet you'd be good at it, too," said the girl.

"Yeah, well," said the lifeguard, and shrugged. "It's hard to keep up, with all I have to do. I study, all right, but it's a temptation to go on out with the other guys."

"It must be," said Rose.

"Oh, yes," said Lansing, softly. He rattled his stick along the railings again, his tray forgotten. When he stands up, I thought, it will fall on the floor.

"I think maybe I will take a walk after all," I said. Lansing's face changed, looked suddenly brighter, hopeful.

"Well, good for you," he said. I took my tray into the kitchen and then stood in the doorway.

"Half an hour? You're quite certain you'll be all right?"

"Of course. I won't move. Where can I go?" I ignored that faint note of irony. I went out the door of the cottage, let the screen door slam behind me, and then crept silently back inside. I sat down in a chair just inside the kitchen door, and watched Lansing. He stood up almost immediately, and the tray slid off his lap and fell on the floor.

"Oh, damnation!" He tapped his way carefully through the mess of plastic dinnerware and spilled food to the porch railing, and then he leaned his stick against his thigh, and stood with his arms on the railing, looking for all the world like any other man staring out to sea in the gathering dusk, a ridiculous cone-shaped straw hat on his head, dark glasses over his eyes.

"I'd better go," said the girl Rose. "Johnny will be asleep by now. The lady in the room next to mine said she'd watch him, but I don't want to leave him too long."

"Gosh, no," said the lifeguard. "Though I guess it's a relief to get a bit of freedom, once in a while."

"It sure is," said Rose. "I'm crazy about that child, but sometimes I get — you know — kind of lonely?"

"I know what you mean," said the lifeguard. "Everyone needs company, once in a while."

"Well, see you tomorrow, Johnny," she said.

"Funny coincidence, his name being the same as mine," said the lifeguard, and they left the beach together, after some foolishness connected with the towel she'd brought to sit on.

The kitchen clock ticked the minutes away. Lansing still stood, apparently staring at the dark sea. Once he pounded the railing with his fist.

"Oh, God," he said, so low I could hardly hear him. "Oh, God." Finally he tapped his way back to his chair, and under cover of that slight noise I went to the screen door, slammed it again, and walked without caution over to him.

"I'm back," I said. "It wasn't very interesting. Just the sand dunes and the thistles."

"I knocked my tray off my lap."

"Yes, quite a mess," I said. "But I'll clean it up. I should have taken it from you, but you hadn't finished eating." How many messes had I cleaned up for Lansing? I got a cloth from the kitchen.

"I ought to look where I'm going," said Lansing, and I looked at him sharply. He hadn't come out with that old joke for years.

"I see our young couple have gone." I was on my knees before him, wiping up spilled milk. "Or have they retreated into the fastness of the sand dunes?"

"They've gone." Lansing tapped his stick on the porch floor once or twice. "You know, I think they'll probably get married." I got to my feet, easily as I always move, despite my age.

"You're too romantic, Lansing. She has a child. He just wants an easy girl, for the summer."

"Sometimes, Mother, you are curiously coarse," said Lansing gently. "This is a real love affair we're being shown. Don't you feel that?"

"*Shown?*" I couldn't help it. Something came out in my voice. There was a long pause. "I think we're talking a lot of nonsense about a couple of cheap youngsters who're after nothing but pleasure," I said finally. "I think we should go to bed. It's quite dark."

"Yes," said Lansing. "It has got dark."

.

They were there the next day, and the next. The conversation was about the same, except that it got more intimate, and the lifeguard sat on the blanket more often. He was neglecting his job, the other lifeguard had to blow the whistle for him to take over the chair. Not that he minded that either, he'd sit there, broiling in the sun, for a long time after it was his partner's turn, and then saunter over to him, laughing, blowing his whistle. Young kids, no sense of responsibility. Lansing's stick rattled on the railings, like a warning of some kind, but the young couple never heeded it. Perhaps they never heard it. Sometimes the child would stop whatever he was doing, and look up for a moment.

"They're playing ball," said Lansing. "Now they're sitting on the sand." It was remarkable how much he could hear, how much he could sense.

"I know it's crazy," said the lifeguard. "I know we've only known each other a few days. But it's true."

"I don't know," she said. "There's Johnny."

"No problem," said the lifeguard. "Honest. I know we can manage. I know we can swing it. Trailers on the campus for married students. I know a couple who — Cute, you know?" After a pause, "Of course, it wouldn't be for long. Just until I get my degree. Then we'd really be swinging."

"I could get a job too," said Rose. "Johnny could go to nursery school."

"Be the best thing in the world for him," said the lifeguard. "He's going to have to get to know other kids, sooner or later. After all, he isn't always going to be — Well. An only child."

.

There had been a storm in the night. The air was clear and fresh, but the waves were still high, and the red flag was up. The lifeguard seemed to have nothing to do, once he'd dug the little boat out of the sand that had washed over it during the storm. Rose was wearing a sweater and slacks, and the baby was in one of those zippered-up affairs, a jacket with a hood attached. They walked hand in hand along the wet beach after a while, with the child trotting after.

"It's the kind of day I like," said Lansing. He too was wearing a sweater; I'd made him put it on, he always caught cold so easily. "This kind of weather. It makes me feel I can do things, somehow."

"What things?"

He tapped his stick impatiently on the floor of the porch. "I don't know. Walk a long way. Run. Dance, even. Get a job, meet more people. How do I know? I've never tried anything."

"It's not your fault," I said. "How could you try what other people do?"

"I don't know," said Lansing. "Sometimes I think I might have."

"I've done everything I could for you, Lansing," I told him. The old worn sentence came out of the rut it had worn in my mind. Always, before, Lansing had been subdued by it. Times he'd wanted to get a job, try things he hadn't the strength for. I know you have, Mother, he would say. I know you have. This time he shrugged, ran his stick along the railings.

"You've dedicated your life to me. I'm not sure it's the best thing you could have done with it. For either of us. It isn't as if you ever had much affection for me."

"How can you — ? What else could I have — ? Just tell me one time when I — " Lansing was silent.

The lifeguard and the girl Rose, with the child wandering behind them, were making their way back, slowly, stopping every two or three minutes to talk, to pick up shells or pebbles. I hated them. Lansing's wonderfully normal young couple, with the perfectly ordinary baby. I watched them walk as far as the lifeguard stand, and lean against it, talking still. Lansing asked me where they were, and I told him.

"Ah, yes," he said. "I can hear them, every minute or so. When the wind blows this way. Only faintly, though. The sea's still making a lot of noise."

"The waves are high." I felt stone cold, with a boiling inside me. The lifeguard suddenly wrapped his arms around the girl, and kissed her. They looked like something in the movies.

"They're kissing," I said, almost spat. "Right out in public."

"It's normal," said Lansing. "There can't be anyone else but us around, not for miles." He kept his face turned toward them, as though he were watching, his expression a strange one, lighted up, pleased. I saw the baby staggering away from his mother, down to the water, stooping to pick up shells on the way.

"Where's the little boy?" said Lansing, suddenly. "Is he with them?"

"He's watching the breakers," I said. I saw the wave touch him, heard his laugh on the wind, watched him run after the foam as it sucked itself down the sand, saw the next breaker catch him and toss him in white water, while his mother stood in the lifeguard's embrace.

"I heard a cry," said Lansing. He stood up abruptly. "Where's the baby, Mother?" he asked. I was filled with a strange excitement.

"He's picking up shells and rubbish," I said. Lansing hesitated for a moment, moving his head as though he were in pain. Suddenly he gave a strange wail, and vaulted the porch railings, and went running, stumbling, across the sand. At the same moment the lifeguard and the girl Rose broke apart and ran down to the water's edge. I saw the lifeguard dive into the next breaker and swim furiously about, looking, and then struggle back for the boat, while Rose wept and wrung her hands. I saw Lansing, running up and down in a curious zig-zag fashion, feeling with obvious terror the nearness, the immensity, of the ocean, shouting words that were brought back to me on the wind.

"The baby, the baby! Where is the baby?"

The Scent of Apples

A BURST OF LAUGHTER from the group on the lawn. Lannie's mother had taken off her hair ribbon, and tied it around the neck of a goose.

"Where's Lannie?" said Mrs. Fox. She sneezed several times, and popped another antihistamine into her mouth. "She ought to see this. Oh dear, how funny!" The goose waddled away, placing its webbed feet far apart, moving its small head from side to side, on the end of the beribboned neck, with the effect of a dowager being gracious in the midst of a mob she couldn't see very well.

"Yes, where *is* Lannie?" That was her mother, looking around, smoothing back her fine dark hair, accepting a rubber band from one of the Munson twins to take the place of her ribbon. No one knew. She hadn't been seen since dinner.

"Old enough to take care of herself. She'll turn up," said her father jovially. A holiday mood, and meant to impress the others. Victorian in some ways, he liked his daughter *there*, and was quite critical of her wandering absences. The Munson twins went off to play cricket, everyone else settled down in the canvas chairs. Lannie in the hayloft scowled blackly, watching them all with hate and a baffled yearning. They had missed her, but they hadn't looked for her. They didn't really care where she was, they were so sure she couldn't come to any harm. I could have fallen off a cliff, for all they know, she thought, forgetful that this kind of absent-minded permission to do as she liked was exactly what she had been aching for. She sat up a little higher in the hay, leaning her head against the side of the loft window. There wasn't much point in hiding, if no one was hunting for her.

The farm lay at the foot of the mountains, a mile from the sea, cloaked in trees, sheltered from the wind, a small Garden of Eden, its own spring bubbling from a pipe set in a rock in the farmyard. Lannie and her parents had been coming here every summer for years. Before writing to Mrs. Mathies, in April, and booking the rooms, they always discussed it at length. Perhaps this year they should do something different. Take a boat, ply up and down the Norfolk Broads. Go to Venice. Take Lannie to Paris, improve her French. There was really nothing to *do* at the farm. You swam, you ate, fished in the lake, climbed Moelfre. But in the end you always came back. The little stream, the steppingstones, the hens who carried their chicks across on fluffed-up, feathered backs; the great dog and the seven-toed kitten — there was *always* a seven-toed kitten — were all familiar. But the people changed, a different group every year. This year, besides Lannie and her parents, there were only the Foxes and the Munsons, Mrs. Fox with her allergies, the Munsons with their detestable twins. Mr. Fox, rather common, made funny little remarks to her that she didn't quite understand. The only bright spot in the holiday so far was the discovery that Mrs. Mathies, the farmer's wife, tired of cats and dogs, horses and cows, and the donkey in the back meadow, had somehow or other acquired a little black monkey she called Nick, who wore an old rhinestone bracelet around his neck for a collar. But even this amusing and exotic addition to the animal life of the farm had ceased to seem very attractive after Lannie discovered he liked no one but his mistress, and chattered angrily at — even bit — anyone else who approached him.

Last year there had been a boy at the farm, but all he was interested in was his motorbike. He'd taken Lannie for a ride; she'd fallen off; her mother — dabbing iodine — scolded her gently and warned her that she must not grow up to be a hoyden, no *nice* boy really liked a rough-and-tumble girl. Lannie had hoped the boy would be at the farm again this summer. Through the growth of something mysterious within herself during the past few months, she had looked forward to the encounter, thought that this time she would not fall off the motorbike. But the boy was gone; all she knew was that his name was Bob. Sometimes she thought of writing him a letter. Dear Bob, I don't suppose you remember me, but I'm the girl who — But there was no address to send it to.

Lannie's mother, fretful at her shyness, noticing that she never invited anyone home from school, suggested that she be more friendly, more outgoing. Lannie wanted to shout, to ask how could she, when her parents treated her so babyishly, dressing her as though she were four, not fourteen, and inviting her, quite formally, to their sherry parties, and taking her to places — museums, art galleries, private views and political meetings — where nothing ever happened and there weren't any boys? But she was too well brought up to do that, and sat in the corner at the last sherry party, as she always did, in her best velveteen, clutching the sherry glass tightly between her fingers, wondering why *she* had to endure miseries like this, when other girls went out with boys and had dances for their friends. "Intellectuals like ourselves . . ." said her parents; and "Standards to keep up . . . great gulf between. The greatest pleasure you will ever get from life will be from . . . *Moby Dick, The Russians.* Of course, the new translations are . . . and Jane Austen." Lannie, watching her mother, watching her dip and sway about the room, sparkling with pleasure and laughter at *her* party, at the success of it, the fun of having so many people gathered together to listen to her and to enjoy themselves, wished she could say, as other girls might, "Ha! You should just see her in her curlers, or early in the morning when she's just got out of bed." But her mother's hair was naturally wavy, thick and fine and glossy, and when she got up in the morning she looked just the same as ever, and usually read a book at breakfast, propping it up against the marmalade pot, waving two fingers in absent-minded farewell to her husband, who went out at eight in the morning, straightening his tie, with a funny self-satisfied look Lannie didn't want to examine.

"You were very quiet, last night," said Lannie's mother. "Didn't you enjoy yourself?" She pulled apart two pages, stuck together with a spot of marmalade.

"It was very nice," said Lannie.

"You shouldn't be so shy," said Lannie's mother. "So withdrawn. You have to come out of yourself more." She shook her head, puzzled, at her daughter, returned to Dostoevski.

Lannie had tried, but it hadn't worked. The other girls

stopped on the corner after school, and talked to the boys from the boys' school a few streets away. They stood there for hours, leaning against the lamppost, books in their arms, school hats pushed carelessly back on their heads. The air was thick with invitations to go roller skating, meet at the zoo, go to the movies. What're you doing Sat aft? Come on over to my house, I've got some new records. My dad's giving me a guitar for Christmas. Lannie stood about awkwardly on the fringes of the group, as bus after bus went by, hoping that someone else would leave before she did. But eventually she was always the first one, jumping on the bus, calling, G'bye, see you tomorrow, barely answered, and not, she was certain, missed in the slightest. Other people's dads gave them guitars for Christmas, but there'd be no such present for Lannie, nothing she could boast about and invite people over to look at and admire, and, if they were very careful, touch. Probably she'd get another velveteen dress, exactly like the one she already had, except that the bodice would be a little more curved, and the lace collar a little smaller. And on Sat aft she had her piano lesson.

"You're filling out so," said Lannie's mother, almost in a complaining tone, when the question of a new velveteen dress came up. "You'll be grown-up before we know it." Grown-up, thought Lannie, in despair, and believed she would never have known what it was like to be young.

Off in the meadow, behind high, overgrown hedges, the Munson twins played cricket, their voices and the sound of the ball on the bat coming queerly, disembodied, in the gathering twilight. They would lose the ball. They always did. Last year, Lannie might have enjoyed their company, baby-sat them with a pleasurable feeling of the difference in ages, but this year she couldn't stand them, and they teased her incessantly. The other day she had saved Christopher from drowning, though as it turned out no one had seemed very impressed. He'd backed away from the donkey he'd been tempting with a celery stalk, fallen into the pond, and been dragged out by Lannie, off on one of her morning walks. He was shrieking with fright and anger, and covered with green slime. She'd hit at his legs with the palm of her hand, as hard as she could, under the pretense of getting the waterweed off him, and then let him go roaring back to the farm alone, the other twin, dawdling, scared, far behind him. Lannie's mother was concerned.

"You might have given a thought to how Mrs. Munson would feel," she said. "Why didn't you take him back yourself, and tell her exactly what happened?"

"Nothing did happen," said Lannie. And then, "I didn't feel like it." How could she explain the fright she herself had had, when she thought Christopher might drown, vanish forever beneath the still, green weed on the surface of the pond, how his hand had shown white, five grasping fingers reaching for the air? She'd been so angry with him when she found he was perfectly all right, only wet and dirty, she'd wanted to punish him, make him go to bed, stay there for a week, his holiday ruined. But he wasn't hers. He was Mrs. Munson's. Mrs. Munson was expecting another baby. That's one thing I'll never do, thought Lannie, drifting away from her mother. I'll never have children. Never. And if it meant she couldn't marry, well, she wouldn't marry either. Probably no one would ask her, in any case.

"They're healthy, though," she heard Mrs. Fox say. "And that's the main thing, isn't it?" Mrs. Munson had been telling her how she felt when Christopher came and said he'd fallen in the pond. Mrs. Munson threw up her hands. She was rather fat, with stout freckled arms, and red hair. She was wearing a pink smock over her dark skirt.

"The things they get up to! Sometimes I'd like to — "

"Ah, but you're so lucky, blessed with children. And — ?" Mrs. Fox paused, delicately.

"Oh, yes." Mrs. Munson patted her stomach. "More to come. I only hope this one won't be twins." She sounded half-regretful, half-pleased.

"But think," said Lannie's mother. "Twin girls! How nice that would be. How suitable. Then you'd have four children for the price, so to speak, of two, and never have to bother again."

"Oh, it's no *bother*," said Mrs. Munson primly. She seemed not to know what to make of Lannie's mother, and subsided into silence. Her husband gave a strange guffaw, and they looked at each other, at a loss. Lannie's mother and father exchanged glances; Lannie's mother laughed, jumped to her feet, and joined Mr. Fox, strolling beyond the boxwoods. Out of sight of the others, but clearly visible to Lannie, they stopped by the peonies. Mr. Fox lighted a cigarette for her, holding a match in his cupped hands. They talked quietly for a while, and then walked back to the others. Lannie's mother flung her half-smoked cigarette away, and one of the chickens dashed for it, clucked disappointedly, and melted into the shadows.

"The moon, the moon," cried Mrs. Fox. She waved thin,

enthusiastic, mosquito-bitten arms to the sky. "Diana the Huntress!" Everyone looked up. For a moment Lannie thought they would look her way, and crouched back in the window.

"So it is," said Lannie's father, and knocked out his pipe. "I think perhaps we ought to — " As though the moon had peculiar powers over him, he rose unsteadily, staggered a little, caught the arm of his wife's chair. "Go in?"

"Oh, John, so early?"

"Well, what then?"

"Let's go for a walk. Just a minute, I'll get my cardigan." She ran into the house, swore vividly and audibly as she tripped, evidently, on the first step of the staircase.

"So young, your wife," said Mrs. Munson, after a pause. "Lovely to have all that energy." She sighed. There had been a faint note of disapproval in her voice. "I think we ought to get the boys," she went on, as though the expletives had somehow contaminated the atmosphere. "Coming, Ted?" The Munson wandered off, around the boxwood hedge.

"You might see if Lannie's with them," called Lannie's father. Mrs. Fox slapped at her arms. She was allergic to everything.

"I think she must have gone to bed," she said. "She was rather gloomy at supper, didn't you think?" She went on, complainingly, "The mosquitoes are frightful. I believe I'll go inside."

"I'll be with you in a minute," said Mr. Fox, sitting in shadow, indifferent. She hovered for a moment or two, collecting her handbag and her knitting needles, her special balsam-filled pillow, and her inhaler. And then she left.

Gloomy at supper, thought Lannie. Was that how it had looked? To herself, it seemed that she had been splendidly aloof, coming from the barn, where she had spent the afternoon — everyone else red and sore from a day on the beach. All the paying guests ate together, feasting really, in the farm dining room, on meats and poultry, vegetables fresh and pickled, blackberry pie with thick cream. Lannie wasn't hungry, had been eating apples all afternoon, but sat there, politely listening to the stupid conversation.

"Mozart, of course," said her father. "Keats. Thomas Chatterton. I don't know." He shook his head. "What are we to do with our children? They seem to cease being children so late."

"Tom Girtin, for that matter," said Lannie's mother. "What did Turner say about him? 'If Girtin had lived, I would have starved.'"

"Rex Whistler," said Mrs. Munson excitedly, getting the idea. "Rupert Brooke. Oh dear." She looked at her children, engaged with rabbit pie, fastidiously placing the pieces of rabbit to the sides of their plates, eating the pastry with grimaces. "One does wonder. Nowadays, they seem to think of nothing but pleasure." She watched her children in wonder, seeing them push the best bits to the side of their plates. The sound of the ball on the bat, the disembodied voices, the lost ball.

"And what does Lannie think?" said Mr. Fox. She couldn't see him very well behind his glasses, but his eyes glinted with a remote interest. He was common, but he had a sense of humor. Was he laughing at her?

"I don't know," she answered, trapped. She didn't like

rabbit either, pushed a piece away with her fork, wishing it
didn't have to taste so winy. The names were almost as
familiar to her as her own. "They all died young, didn't they?
I mean, they stopped being grown-up rather quickly. They
died. They all died." To her surprise, everyone burst out
laughing, even the Munson twins, punching each other's arms.

"Lannie, you're a marvel!"

"The young — "

"Right to the heart of the — "

"Out of the mouth — "

Lannie excused herself quickly; they were all being so self-
congratulatory, they wouldn't notice. She went to the barn,
making a face at the little black monkey in his cage in the
hall, who seemed to make a face back, and climbed the ladder
to the loft, speaking to the horses till they calmed down,
stopped their stamping and blowing, and became still, and
she could hear the chirping of the baby chicks that pecked at
the straw beneath their feet.

"All right, dear, here I am," said Lannie's mother, coming
out of the house wearing, as Lannie saw with silent rage, one
of Lannie's own cardigans, the rose red one she'd bought with
her own money. Lannie's father hauled himself up from the
canvas chair, they lighted cigarettes, coughed, talked for a
moment, and went off along the path and through the gate.
The dog followed them, whined, scratched, and lifted a leg.

"If you see Lannie, tell her to go to bed," called Lannie's
mother.

"Right," said Mr. Fox. Lannie felt a moment's panic.
She knew she couldn't get to her bedroom without anyone
seeing her. Did Mr. Fox matter? He sat there, glowing cigarette end illuminating a patch of white shirt.

"Why don't you come along?" said Lannie's father, ghostly on the other side of the gate.

"No, thanks, quite comfortable where I am."

The Munsons trailed across the lawn, making for the golden rectangle marking the farmhouse door, dragging their protesting children.

"Early to bed, early to rise," said Mr. Munson. "We'll go to the beach tomorrow."

"Can I take my fins? My goggles? Please?" The door banged, the golden rectangle was no more, there was silence, broken suddenly by a series of protesting quacks and honks from the direction of the pond. The other geese don't like the ribbon, thought Lannie. They think it makes her too different from the rest of them. She reached behind her and took an apple, waiting for what would happen.

The day before, she had routed the Munson twins, who had discovered the barn, and spent a happy fifteen minutes throwing the apples out of the window. Lannie had kicked their shins with her sandaled feet until they howled, and scrambled down the ladder to safety.

"Yah, you're a girl! Can't fight fair!" shouted one of them. Not Christopher, the other one. "Just you wait!"

"You'd better not come up here again," said Lannie. "I'll kill you if you do. This is my place." And they had vanished, and not come up since. Lannie picked bits of apple from between her teeth with the nail of her little finger, thinking that it was *her* place. Hay, and the sweet gloom, no matter what the time of day, the odd pieces of leather and brass hanging on nails around the walls. A pitchfork leaning against a beam, and now and then a soft scurrying. Mice in the hay, birds in the eaves.

Someone was whistling in the garden. "My Lady Green-sleeves," once an almost forgotten song, this year so popular you could hear it all day long if you wanted to, if you had a transistor radio, which Lannie hadn't. What a drip, she thought, following a shadow until it paused beneath the loft window. There was a sudden spinning of a glowing cigarette end into a flower bed.

"You're supposed to be upstairs," said Mr. Fox.

"How did you know I was here?" said Lannie. She took another bite of apple, leaned out of the window.

"I saw you come up," said Mr. Fox. "You've been here all along." She couldn't see him with any distinctness, as he stood on the shadowed path, but she suddenly became conscious that she herself was illuminated by the moonlight, arms and hands and the top of her head brilliantly lighted, only her face in darkness, beneath a fall of hair. She pushed her hair back, lifted her head affectedly.

"The moon, the moon," she mocked, pleasantly conscious of being rude but out of reach. "Diana, the Huntress!"

"You know what you're doing up there, don't you?" said Mr. Fox.

"No. What am I doing?" said Lannie. She was instantly filled with guilt, was terrified at what he might say. The mysterious power that had come to her earlier in the summer flooded through her now. She stroked her hair on one side of her face, pressing it to her cheek, fingering the ends. Split. She'd have to get her mother to let her have a permanent. She was quite sure, for the first time, that she could overcome her mother's objections. She leaned over the sill of the hayloft window and repeated, "Well, what am I doing?"

"Spying."

"I'm not," crowed Lannie. She threw the apple core so that it would just miss him. "I'm eating apples."

"You ought to be spanked," said Mr. Fox. "I've got a good mind to come up and do it." There was a long questioning silence.

"Just as you like," said Lannie, heady with excitement and power. "They've got wild horses down there. I can tell you, they're dangerous."

"All right," said Mr. Fox. He had lighted another cigarette, but he crushed it beneath his heel. "Here I come." Wretchedly she groped for an apple. It was always as well to be doing something, when grownups appeared. She chewed rapidly and nervously until Mr. Fox loomed at the head of the ladder, disheveled, rumpled, moonlight flashing off his glasses.

"What a lovely hiding place," he said. "And what a marvelous scent of apples. Where are they?"

"Over here. You can't see them in the dark. Here, catch." She got up and tossed him one. He caught it clumsily, staggering on the hay. Lannie went back to her place, took the pitchfork from the wall, and leaned on it negligently.

"Delicious. But wrinkled and wizened. Last year's. They ought to feed them to the pigs."

"You don't know much about the farm," said Lannie, scornfully. "They don't keep pigs. Anyway, they're good. Eat it."

"Is that all you do here?" he asked, his mouth moving. "Eat apples?"

"There isn't much else." Her voice was full of sorrow, for the empty days of the summer. Mr. Fox bounded over the

hay toward her, a gigantic cherub over a sea of clouds. He
was beside her looking out of the loft window, his arm laid
familiarly over her shoulders.

"Except spying," he said. "I saw you, when your mother
and I . . ."

"I can't help it, if people keep coming and going," she said
hotly, leaning on the pitchfork.

"Of course not. I didn't mean anything." She had sounded
hotter than she meant; he looked at her anxiously. He removed his arm from her shoulders, sat down at her feet. "Got
pretty ankles, did you know that?" He was staring at her legs.

"Pretty? Well, I don't know," said Lannie. "I've got lots
of scars. I fell off my bike. There's that one. And then when
we went to the zoo one day, I was about six or seven, and I
tried to climb the fence to the lions' cage. It'll never heal.
Not properly. See how red it is? It'll always be like that."
She was proud of the lions' cage one. "And then one day I
tried to climb up on the milk cart. I should have had
stitches . . ."

"Yes, yes," said Mr. Fox. "Lovely legs. You could win a
beauty contest with them; had you ever thought of that?"

"A beauty contest?" In the village there'd been girls who
stuck their legs through holes in a canvas. That was the
closest she'd come, and she hadn't been much impressed.

"A beauty contest. They had one in the village. The girls
stuck their legs through holes in a canvas. They weren't any
of them as pretty as you." He slipped his arm behind her
knees, she went down, slithered, scrambled. He pressed his
face close to hers. She was hideously frightened, felt as though
she were drowning. With both hands she clutched the pitch-

fork, low down on the handle, and jabbed him in the chest. He sat upright, on the note of a faint scream. Two spots of blood, wide apart, black in the moonlight, appeared startlingly on his white shirt. Flowering blossoms of blood, around the small tears in the fabric.

"I don't know how you're going to explain that," he said, looking down, dabbing with his thumb. "I really don't." She'd never hit a grownup before, much less stabbed one. She looked with horror and repugnance at the two marks.

"But I'm not going to have to, am I?" she said, white, her lips and tongue suddenly quite numb. "I mean, I'm not the one who got stabbed." Mr. Fox got awkwardly to his feet, bunched his coat front about him.

"You should have been," he said. "You were asking for it, all right. If you say one word about this. Just one word."

"I won't say anything," said Lannie, very fast. "Don't you think you ought to put something on that? Iodine, or something?"

"Oh, I will," said Mr. Fox. "Don't you worry. I will."

She watched him go down the path to the house, hurrying, a little hunched over, trying to look as though he were not hurrying, as though he had all the time in the world. Sighing, she released her grip on the pitchfork, put it carefully back in its place against the wall. She buried her face in the hay, cried for a long time, silently, her shoulders heaving. Finally it was over, and she sat up, went down the ladder and into the house. Nick, the monkey, had been asleep, but leaped to the front of his cage as she went by, rhinestone collar glimmering. He bared his teeth at her.

"Little beast," she said. "Beastly. Beastly. I hate you."

She ran up to her own room, to lie there trembling until her parents came back from their walk. Laughing, they came down the corridor, ran the bath water, closed a door behind them.

"Lannie," she heard her mother say, just before the latch clicked. "My goodness, she's growing up so!" And Lannie lay there, curled up, feeling small, infinitesimally small and ugly, wishing she could die young.

The Girl on the Beach

RON CARRIED THE PICNIC BASKET, the blanket, the folding chairs, the inflatable plastic wading pool, and the beach umbrella. Quite far ahead of him, the two women, each holding a child by the hand, made their way among the family groups on the beach, looking for a place to sit.

It was always the same on the first day. There was always the same anxious casting about for the exactly right spot to sit in, some restless, driving instinct impelling the women on for perhaps two hundred yards from the wooden stairs leading down from the boardwalk to the sand.

Two hundred yards at least, thought Ron, and all this gear to carry back again. They were watching him, his wife, Muriel, and her sister Ellen, still holding tightly to the children's hands. Both boys were pulling and tugging in the direction of the water. Even Joey, Ron saw, though he'd never be allowed in, pulling angrily. But the women stood immovable, their heavy white legs planted in the sand like the four legs of a large animal. Their two heads turned slowly toward each other, and Ron imagined that their eyes rolled, expressing a mutual exasperation and impatience at the sight of him staggering under his load, the beach umbrella slipping from his grasp, one end of the blanket trailing so that he stepped on it twice and almost fell.

"Come *on*, Ron," called his wife. "It'll be time to turn around and go back before we get the umbrella up, at this rate." Silently he came up to them, and put everything down except the umbrella, which he opened. He hated the umbrella, for some reason. Perhaps because of its ugly, rusty green and brown stripes. It looked depressingly shabby besides the gayer ones all around, with their flowered linings. Perhaps because he had carried it so far, so many summers. Perhaps because he knew he didn't cut the best of figures, standing with his thin legs straddled and braced, his hair, badly cut, lusterless and graying, falling over his eyes as he drove the pointed wooden stick into the sand with a certain angry energy, and swung it backward and forward until it had gone deep enough and would hold.

He unfolded the beach chairs, and stood them side by side in the shade of the umbrella, and spread the faded cotton blanket out for the children. Muriel and Ellen lowered themselves into the chairs, and the two boys stood with their heads twisted around, away from their mother, gazing at the edge of the water, where crowds of children darted ceaselessly, like minnows in the shallows.

"Can't you let go of them now?" said Ron.

"All right, just as soon as you've got the pool inflated," said Muriel. "Here, Ellen, let me have Billy. Sit down right here, Billy. Your father's going to get your pool ready for you." Ellen relinquished Billy's hand, and the boy sat down obediently at his mother's feet.

Puffing his cheeks and forcing air through the plastic tube,

Ron watched as the child picked up a handful of sand and let it trickle through his fingers, looking up at his mother with a gentle placid smile, lit up with a glorious glow from the sun, beneath his white linen hat. Muriel was right. There was no denying that Billy was an easy child to get along with. Docile, biddable, always did what you told him to without any fuss, always able to amuse himself. There was a lot to be said for Billy. Yet Ron turned his eyes with relief to his other son. Joey stood, mutely angry and obstinate, his heavy dark face — he gets that from me, thought Ron — sullen and mutinous. He made no effort to get away from his mother, whose hand was still grasping his arm, but he fidgeted and shuffled, and kicked the aluminum leg of Ellen's chair.

"Don't do that, Joey," said Ellen, but hopelessly, as though she knew it was no good talking to Joey; he was bound on his own bad ends, and something would have to be done about him. She took out her knitting, and began to count stitches.

Ron finished with the pool, and put it down in front of Billy and stood up.

"Come on, Joey," he said. "Bring your pail, and we'll get the water."

"He'll only get all wet," said Muriel.

"What's he come to the beach for?" said Ron. "Come on, Joey."

"That cabana set is brand-new," said Muriel. "I don't want him getting it soaked. He can play in the sand, like Billy. You get the water." She exerted pressure with her strong wrist, and forced Joey down to a sitting position beside her. When she released him, he took off his hat and threw it some distance from him, as though in revenge.

"I hate that hat," he said. "I'm not going to wear it." Ellen

struggled forward in her deck chair, as though to retrieve it.
On vacation, Joey was her cross, as Billy was his mother's,
though not enjoyed and not lightly borne. She leaned back
again, as Ron picked the hat off the sand.

"You'd better put it back on," said Muriel. "You ought to
have a hat on, in this sun."

"It's a stupid hat," said Joey. "It's a girl's hat. I'm not
going to wear it."

"I don't think he needs it," said Ron. "None of the other
kids seem to be wearing them." He turned it in his hands.
It *was* a girl's hat. White linen, like Billy's, but with a pattern
of red and blue daisies. "There are flowers on it," he said
accusingly. He'd thought they must be flags, or little trucks,
or animals, but now he could see they were little bunches of
flowers. Joey was wearing a short white linen jacket over his
white swimming trunks, and Ron noticed the lining of the
jacket matched the hat.

"Why not?" said Muriel. "He's only a child. Nobody
notices those things."

Except you, who do those things on purpose, thought Ron.

"He's eight. A bit too old for flowered bonnets." He
looked at Billy, who was patting the edge of the empty pool,
and murmuring urgently. He clenched the hat in his hand,
and held it close to his side.

"Stop fussing, Ron. Go and get the water. Can't you see
Billy wants his pool filled up?"

Ron took the plastic pail and stumbled through the soft
sand where they were sitting to the hard, damp sand close to
the water. He stood up looking up and down the beach, with
a sudden feeling of refreshment and ease. For miles in either

direction, a frieze of happy children played, their swimsuits little points of bright color, dotted thickly all over the sand and in the surf, more thinly in the water beyond the white line of the breakers. Beach balls flew, red and white. Inflatable rubber rafts, emerald green and yellow, bobbed on the water. The ocean swelled and moved, a great tame beast in whose beard the children played. White and gray seagulls dipped down and flew up again. For miles in either direction, under the gay striped and flowered beach umbrellas, happy parents watched their happy children. Who can look at the sea and not be calmed?

Ron glanced back at Muriel and Ellen, sitting in their chairs. Even with his glasses on, it was hard to see that far. A navy blue blob with dark hair was Muriel. A magenta blob with gray hair was Ellen. He tried to keep his mind as pleasantly neutral as he hoped he usually kept his face, but as he waded into the water the small thought slipped in and inscribed itself: Ugly women, in ugly clothes.

He dipped the pail as a wave came in, and when he straightened up his glasses were flecked with foam. For a moment he stared, startled, into an irridescent, sparkling world, of a million tiny bubbles, before he lifted his hand to wipe them away.

"Hey, Dad," said Joey, beside him. "Where's my hat?"

"So you got away, did you? I dropped it in the water. There was a wave, didn't you see? I got splashed all over. I felt as if I'd got lost in a washing machine." Joey took his hand.

"You dropped it on purpose, didn't you?"

"I didn't take the greatest possible care of it," he admitted.

"Where is it now?" said Joey. They looked at the water swirling about their legs, and a small girl in an enormous bathing cap of pink rubber flower petals flopped between them like a stranded fish. She was swept away again in a moment, laughing and tumbling.

"I don't know," said Ron. "Perhaps a crab's got it." Joey hopped on one leg with pleasure.

"A crab is wearing my stupid old hat!" he shrieked, and gave Ron a push that took him by surprise. He went down into the water, as the next wave came, and felt the pebbles and shells pounding about him. Sand poured over him. He held his breath and came up gasping, holding on to his glasses, his hair sleek and wet over his forehead. He saw Joey swept away from him by the undertow, and was assailed by a moment's panic. He's a big boy, his mind told him rapidly. He'll be all right.

"Watch it, Joey," he called, and Joey, as the wave broke over him, was swept right by his father's feet. He lay there, with his elbows digging into the sand, water streaming off him, laughing up at his father, and Ron was assailed by such a rush of love and affection and happiness that he could have wept. He brushed his wet hair off his face, and took off his glasses, to wipe them on the corner of his shirt, and heard Ellen.

"Muriel says you're to bring the water for Billy's pool, and quit fooling around. Joey, you're a bad boy. Look at you. Soaking wet, and you're still wearing your jacket. Your mother wants you to come up to her right now."

They followed her up the beach, silently. Joey tried to catch Ron's eye, but Ron avoided his look. He was staring at

Ellen. Magenta elasticized swimsuit, bulging white thighs. Gray curls. Her legs moved determinedly one after the other, her elbows pumped, her face was beginning to get red because of the heat. What fools we must look, thought Ron, tiredly. All except Joey. A miserable little procession of two, Ellen followed by himself, grasping a child's pail in one hand, too thin, too awkward, too gangly, also white, wearing glasses, his wet suit flapping on him. Joey drifted along behind them — Ron assured himself with a quick glance — humble in posture, unabashed at heart, laughing to himself at the idea of a crab wearing the hideous and feminine hat.

"Look at your cabana set," said Muriel furiously. Ellen subsided into her chair, and took up her knitting. "Just look at it. Soaking wet, and full of sand." Ron looked down at himself. Muriel had given him the outfit for his birthday. The shirt and swim shorts matched. A yellowy green, printed with a pattern of snowcapped mountains, herons flying, and little men in coolie hats fishing in waterfalls. Idiots, thought Ron, and wiped the word out of his mind immediately, because of Billy. He emptied the pailful of water into Billy's pool, and lifted the child into it.

"I'll get some more. Come on, Joey," he said, and turned to go back to the water. Billy patted the bottom of the pool, sending up little splashes.

"Not with Joey," said Muriel. "Joey's been a bad boy. He's going to have to stay here with me."

"I haven't been bad," said Joey truculently.

"Oh yes you have," said Ellen, looking up from her knitting. "You ran away from your mother. A nice boy doesn't do that."

Madame Defarge, thought Ron, waiting for the heads of the children.

"I'll get some more water," he said. "Joey's all right. He just fell, that's all. His jacket will dry."

"He was naughty," said Muriel. "And he'll have to be punished. No ice cream tonight. No candy."

Billy patted the half-inch of water he sat in, making little splashes, cooing like a dove.

"Oh, come on," said Ron. "Let Joey come down to the water with me. I promise you, we won't swim. We'll just fill the pail."

"Nice boys don't run away from their mothers," said Muriel, and Ellen nodded over her knitting. People were beginning to stare at them.

"All right," said Ron. He went down to the breakers alone, and filled the pail, and when he'd done it three or four times the pool was full, and Billy dabbled his fingers in it and smiled cheerfully at his parents and his aunt.

"He's the best boy in the world," said Muriel, and touched his face with the back of her hand. "Ron, move the umbrella so Billy gets some shade. I think he's getting too hot."

.

None of them went near the water again. Joey lay on his stomach and kicked sand disconsolately, and was rebuked. Ron sat in the sun with a towel over his head and stared out to sea. All around them an extraordinarily vivid and energetic life seemed to be going on, so close that it could literally be touched. Yet here they sat in a strange magic circle, under a spell that prevented them from being happy. And no one knew. As far as anyone else was concerned, they were all but invisible, just another family party, sitting quietly. No one noticed how long and how quietly they sat. No one noticed that they hadn't all just come running up the sand, laughing and flinging drops of water, or that they never went running down the sand and splashed into the sea, a little frieze of pleasure of their own.

"Why don't I take some pictures?" said Ron. He got the camera out of the picnic basket. Amateur photography was his hobby. He had some wonderful shots of the children. That was what he told people. He only half realized it was Joey who was his hobby, that he had taken up photography so he could catch Joey in a tree, grinning incongruously through the blossoms, Joey playing ball in the yard — alone, since Muriel wouldn't let him play with the neighborhood kids — Joey riding a bicycle, alone of course, and in the yard, since Muriel didn't like him to take it in the street. But reasonably content, and normally vigorous. The camera was a way of enjoying Joey more, and longer. He focused on him now, moving the camera slightly so as to exclude Muriel's legs.

"Hey, Joey," he said, and as Joey looked up, frowning, Ron took the picture. Then Joey smiled.

"Hold it," said Ron, and took another one.

"Take some of Billy," said Ellen, dropping her knitting. "He looks so cute, sitting there like that." Ron, scrupulously fair, took two of Billy. All the pictures of Billy were the same, he thought, moving his position to take the several shots of Ellen and Muriel that would only be polite. Billy was smiling and placid in all of them, beaming at the camera. Up until a year or so ago, you hardly saw there was anything wrong with him, hardly noticed the funny, half-finished movements of his hands, the funny, half-finished look of the lower part of his face. Of course, to hear Muriel tell it, there wasn't anything wrong with him. For Muriel, Billy was the perfect child. Since Billy was about four, though, Ron had had to be reminded to photograph him. Since then, he thought, the smile had been obviously mindless, the beaming glance distressingly arch. In a photograph you saw it at once, where at first glance at Billy himself you might miss it.

"All right, ladies," he said. "Say cheese." As he took the picture, someone came running between them, laughing. A girl in a sea-blue swimsuit, fair hair flying. Ron collapsed on his haunches, expecting her to be followed by a boy, another girl, a whole troupe of young people, the kind that ran along the beach sometimes, the flying sand from their footprints stinging your eyes and ruining your lunch. You followed them with your eyes until they ran into the breakers, and then you straightened out the blanket they had heedlessly run across, shook out the towels, buried the ruined sandwich, and took another, warily, from wax-paper wrappings, knowing they would be back again, or another troupe like them. Half-annoyed, half-envious, thinking vaguely they looked like figures on a Greek vase, you took another sandwich. But no one followed the girl in the blue suit.

"I don't think that will come out," said Ron. "I'd better take some more." He wondered, as he took his generous series of pictures of Muriel and Ellen, what the girl had been laughing about, running all alone on the beach.

·

Later, in the evening, they walked on the boardwalk. Up

there it was noisy and hot, and dirty. The boards, resounding under hundreds of pairs of feet, were littered with popcorn, caramels, chewing gum, spilled ice cream and paper cups. Ron would rather have walked along the dusky sand with Joey. The tide was out; they might have found some shells, a beached fish, crabs, anything. The boardwalk was brilliantly lighted, the sea shut out as effectively as though curtains had been drawn.

They walked on the boardwalk. Past the taffy-making machine, the postcards, the swimsuits, the balloons, past the bowling alley and the amusement park. Ellen and Muriel were wearing white cotton blouses, the sleeves too short over their bulging upper arms, and dark cotton skirts, printed with brimming cocktail glasses and bubbles in green and red.

Muriel hadn't been able to find Ron's slacks, and for a horrible moment he thought he must have lost his clothes.

"Wear your cabana set," she said.

"Do they let you? On the boardwalk? Aren't there some rules?"

"It's perfectly decent," she said. "A shirt and a pair of shorts. Nobody could object to that. So what? They match." But it wasn't that. It was the horrible greeny yellow color of them, the somehow effeminate pattern of snowcapped mountains and little men fishing in waterfalls. Fortunately he found his slacks in the closet. He'd put all his things away himself. Pleased with himself, decently clad in dark trousers and a white shirt, his hair brushed, after an I-don't-look-too-bad-after-all glance at the mirror he slapped Muriel's bottom. She was pulling on her skirt, bending over. She looked at him with outrage in her eyes.

"Sorry," he said nervously. "Just feeling my oats." He went

out quickly, and waited for her downstairs, where Ellen and the children were already stamping impatiently. But he could not dismiss the moment from his mind. Muriel called love-making a marital duty, or marital relations, when she referred to it at all. Ron knew she considered him disgusting for his part in the performance of such duty. He knew she could not bear any contemplation of such relations. She was prudish and uncharitable, he thought, as he gazed into a display of shells cleverly put together to represent animals and clowns. Behind him, Ellen scolded Joey, and held Billy up so he wouldn't fall. But he should have known it from her appearance, Ron told himself. The receding chin, the teeth exposed like those of a bad-tempered mare, the suspicious glance, the stiff and dated curls of her black hair. But the poor woman. She had a secret, and one that Ron would never give away. Prudish and uncharitable as she was, she had a part too to play in the marital duty, and her disgust at Ron was as much for the times when he did not act, as for the times when he did. Somehow they never came together pleasantly and hap-pily. Lust took them by surprise, and separately. One or the other of them was always the unwilling and shamed aggressor, one or the other the unwilling and shamed victim. He won-dered for the thousandth time, as the shadowy reflections of Ellen and his two sons played in the glass he stared at, why he had married her. She had trapped him very simply, but he never faced the fact, and always tried to dredge up a reason, something that would excuse him, and save him from considering himself as mindless and foolish as Billy.

Muriel came down at last, and they walked on the board-walk, right to where the boardwalk ended. There were just a few beach houses, half-hidden by the dunes; the noise of the more crowded section was heard faintly. There was a bench placed there, right where the boardwalk ran into the sand and was finished. There was the last bench, and the last overhead light, and then miles and miles of the mysterious nighttime beach. A girl sat on the bench. She was quite alone. She had long, fair hair, of a curious paleness, tied somehow in a careless knot at the back of her head, long strands of it escaping and blowing about her face. She wasn't exactly looking out to sea, but her head was tilted slightly as though she were listening to it. She was wearing a blue and white dress, with long sleeves. In the breeze the material rippled slightly.

"Waiting for someone," said Muriel disapprovingly.

"Long sleeves, on a night like this?" said Ellen.

There wasn't any way in which he could get a better look at her. The boardwalk quite obviously ended there, just where she sat. They all turned around and began to walk back again. Ron was sure she was the girl who had worn the blue bathing suit.

.

On the way back to the hotel, they stopped at various stores. Saltwater taffy was being made in one. Ron held Billy up, so he could see. Joey pressed close beside him. Billy may not have appreciated the machinery, but he was ecstatic at the scent of peppermint and vanilla.

"A two-pound box," said Muriel. She gave a piece to Billy, unwrapping it for him and letting the paper fall among the rest of the litter about their feet.

"Me too," pleaded Joey.

"No. Remember what I said? No candy, and no ice cream. You were a bad boy today."

"Bad for your teeth, anyway," said Ron quietly.

They stopped to look at postcards outside a store advertising a sale of beach wear. After a long time spent in spinning the stand around, and discarding one card after another, the two women went into the store with Billy. Ron and Joey went to the railings of the boardwalk and stood with their arms folded on it, looking out at the dark sea. On the horizon lights flickered. There were ships. One light was larger than the rest, and steady.

"The Jersey shore," said Ron.

"Yeah? Truly?" Joey stared hard.

"It's not a foreign country, you know," said Ron, amused. "I'll show you a map." Below them, beneath the boardwalk, there were giggles, and a sudden flurry of movement. Ron had seen the four youngsters run silently in among the pilings, among the broken beer bottles and into the dank ammonia smell of the dark.

"What are they doing?" said Joey.

"Fooling around. Making love." Joey squatted down and peered between the cracks in the boards, as interested as he had been at the taffy-making machine.

"Joey! Get up!"

"I just wanted to see how they made it," he said, straightening up.

"I shouldn't have said that," said Ron. "That isn't how you make it. They're just kids. Children. Having a good time."

"That girl," said Joey. "She looked kind of like a mermaid, didn't she?" Ron looked at him, startled.

"What girl?" Joey shrugged impatiently.

"*That* girl. The one we saw. Back there, sitting on that seat." Oh yes, *that* girl, thought Ron. Botticelli. The fantastic cords of yellow hair, the pale oval face.

"Yes, I suppose she did. Maybe it was the blue dress." There was an odd silence between them. "Let's go and see what Mother and Aunt Ellen are doing."

.

In the beach-wear shop, Ellen and Muriel were leaning over a counter, looking at a lace tablecloth. Billy, half-asleep, leaned against his mother's side. Joey went over to join them. There was a sale going on. All kinds of things were displayed in open boxes. Ron fingered a terrycloth bathrobe, white, piped in scarlet. Rough to the touch, yet masculine, and somehow comforting and reassuring. A take-a-hot-bath-and-go-to-bed sort of coziness about it. He looked up at his wife and sister-in-law, half-intending to tell them he thought he'd get the bathrobe. They had moved to another counter. They were bent over a selection of silk-rayon robes for men. The saleswoman shook out one, a peculiarly ugly slate blue, with a dragon embroidered on the back in gold thread.

"That's fine," said Muriel. "What do you think?" She was speaking to Ellen.

"Perfect," said Ellen. "Distinguished-looking. Ron will just love it."

"Well, I don't know if he'll love it or not," said Muriel,

"but he can use another robe. It'll make a good Christmas gift."

Ron went out of the store as she made the purchase. He was spinning the postcard stand around when they finally emerged.

.

In the morning Ron was awakened early by the sound of the screen door being very gently closed. He lay still for a moment and listened. Muriel lay beside him. Billy, who always slept in the room with them, was lying on his back, his arms flung out, his face flushed and pink, his hair in damp curls on his forehead. He looked, Ron thought, like a truculent yet angelic dictator, asleep, ready for anyone, dreaming of the ones he had conquered already. And yet when he sat up, he would whimper and whine — the early morning was the only time he was fretful — his pajamas would be soaked, and by the time he was washed and dressed his urgent need for breakfast would be conveyed by murmurings and bangings and anxious looks. His lower lip, pushed out redly in sleep, would be plucked back beneath his upper teeth, his fingers would splay out like restless starfish. Ron sighed. He could hear Ellen snoring gently across the hall. It was Joey who had gone out. The little devil, he thought, and slipped from Muriel's side. He began to dress quickly. The things closest to hand were the shorts and shirt of his cabana set, and for once he didn't think of what an ugly color they were, nor how he hated the design. He thrust his feet into a pair of beach sandals, ran his fingers through his hair, and left, as quietly as Joey had.

There was no sign of the boy on the street. Only a few people were about, mostly elderly, moving slowly and majestically on rented bicycles. Ron ran toward the beach, and looked up and down the boardwalk. Then he went down the wooden steps to the sand, and made for the part where it was damp and hard. Where would I go, if I were Joey? He started to the left, where there were fewer houses and hotels, and where after a few minutes he would come to the sand dunes and pine trees. The sea lay calm and almost flat, swelling gently as though under oil. There was a faint mist over the water. Early as it was, there were naked footprints in the sand, along the line of the tide. Shell hunters. The big hotel was shuttered and quiet. It would be several hours before the beach boys started putting out the striped cabanas, and serving drinks. Where was Joey? Quite close to shore, a pair of porpoises rose and plunged, sleekly black and shining, making their lazy, playful way down the coast. I must tell Joey I saw that, thought Ron.

The girl sat on a breakwater, in the same blue swimsuit she had worn the day before, with an open zippered jacket over it, and her hair tied up in a white scarf, one strand escaping and blowing out over her face. She looked out to sea, swinging one bare foot. Following the line of her leg as though it were a pointer on a map, Ron saw Joey, crouched at her feet, examining something he held in his cupped hands.

"Joey!" he cried. "I've been looking for you!" Joey looked up.

"I've got a sand crab," he said. "Come and see." Ron bent down and looked. The creature, pale shelled, yet somehow naked, wriggled on his son's hand.

"Throw it away," he said. "Let it go, into the ocean."

"'He likes the way it tickles," said the girl. Ron looked at her, startled. "Didn't you ever collect things, when you were a little boy?"

"Lord yes." He smiled.

"Well then." She took off her jacket. "Let's swim."

"I can't swim," said Ron. "Joey can't either."

"I'll teach you," she said. They looked at her doubtfully.

"It's all right. I can swim like a fish. Watch." She ran into the water and swam. Her naked arms flickered, and her hair streamed. Her feet broke the water like the twin fins of a tail. She stood up, the water breast high, and waved to them to join her.

"See! I'll show you how. Joey first." Joey looked at his father. After a moment Ron nodded, and Joey ran to meet the girl. She laid him on his stomach, supporting his chest with her hand, and talked to him. He floundered about and sank. She talked some more, and his movements took on a pattern. After a while she came up to the sand with him.

"He'll know how in a couple of days," she said. "He isn't a bit afraid. How about you?" He felt foolish, and was about to refuse, but Joey pulled at him.

"Go on, Dad." He took off his shirt. It took him a few moments to nerve himself to do it, but after the initial shock of entry he found the water quite warm, and stood beside the girl in the gentle swell of the sea, smoothing his hair with his hand and smiling at her in a mixed way, partly as though she were a schoolteacher he had to placate, partly as though he were the schoolteacher, and she one of his grown-up students, and a little bit as though he had just been introduced to her by Muriel at the A & P. He could not, however, recognize her as safe, for she had no grocery cart protectively in front of her, to proclaim her status as a domestic one, to declare to the world a mystic pregnancy, in which the cart, filled with goods bought with her husband's money, would, by definition, soon be occupied by a baby. Here they stood, Ron and the girl in the blue swimsuit, dangerously free and divided only by green water, which was no division at all.

"You're still wearing your glasses," she accused. He took them off and waved them about ineffectually, wondering where to put them, before he went back and laid them down on top of his shirt.

"Watch my glasses," he told Joey, as though someone might steal them, or as if he thought they might arch up and go walking off by themselves on their long, thin legs. Joey, absorbed by the sand crabs, nodded, not looking up.

The touch of the girl's hand on his chest was extraordinary. It frightened him, so that he floundered and sank, rearing away from her hand rather than from the water.

"Breathe in, put your head down, breathe out, turn your head to the side, breathe in," she said.

"Move your arms. Not like that. Like this. Kick," she said. All the time her hand was flat against his chest. Something happened; a pattern developed. Her hand was gone, and he sank and spluttered and came to the surface again. Something trailed across his face and he clutched at it in a panic, scratching his nose with his fingernail. Her hair. She was floating beside him, waiting for him to be ready to try again. They did it over and over.

"I guess I'm too old," he said ruefully. She looked at him in surprise.

"You're doing fine. You, and Joey too. Come back tomor-

row. I'll be here waiting." They went up on the beach, and
the girl put her jacket on and tied her hair up in the scarf.

"We're all wet," said Joey. "What are we going to do?"
His dismayed voice brought back the presence of Muriel and
Ellen, of Billy eating his breakfast, of the green and brown
umbrella.

"Run along the sand," said the girl. "You'll dry off in a
minute. That's what I'm going to do. Run all the way home."
She waved and ran, and they stood and watched her bare legs
glittering along the sand. Ron wondered where she was going,
but she ran until she was a small blue dot on the beach, and
still had not turned up toward any of the houses and beach
cottages. They looked at each other hesitantly. Ron put on
his shirt and his glasses.

"Race you, Dad," said Joey suddenly, and they ran too, in
the opposite direction.

.

Muriel made no comment when Ron explained they had felt
like going for a walk before breakfast, other than shrugging
as though what they did defied her understanding, and saying,
"Better you than me," as though they had undertaken a chore
she was glad to have been spared.

They spent the next days on the beach exactly as they always did, though now Ron knew how far down he would have
to carry the umbrella and the rest of the stuff. Occasionally
they saw the girl in the blue suit, running along the beach, but
she never came near them, though once Ron waved covertly
at her, and she seemed to wave back. Sometimes at night
they saw her sitting on the last bench on the boardwalk, but

they never spoke to her, though if her face was turned toward
them Ron would smile at her, and she smiled discreetly back
and turned away. He wondered at Joey's duplicity. He
thought often that Joey might run up and speak to her, but
he never did, seeming to understand that she was a secret
between the two of them.

In the mornings they swam with her in the fresh, clean sea.
It didn't take long, she was right; they learned quickly, and in
three or four days they were rolling and spinning in the water
like three porpoises. Ron felt she understood his difficulties,
having seen him so often with the two ungainly women and
the retarded Billy, and the feeling made his manner with her
increasingly easy and free. He thought he was falling in love
with her, and had fantastic dreams of making love to her out
there, in the deep water. He and Joey both got tanned, and
seemed stronger. He'd never been so happy in his life.

On their last day, Ron told her they were leaving.

"Too bad," she said. "But it's the way vacations are. I'll
be going too, at the end of next week."

"We won't be going till about four," he said. "Maybe I'll
see you on the beach, before then."

"I'm a mother's helper," she said regretfully. "This is the
only time of day I have to myself. I hardly ever get down to
the beach, even. Most of the time I teach a bunch of kids
swimming, in the motel pool. Imagine swimming in chlori-
nated water, with all this beautiful ocean in front of us? But
their mother thinks it's safer."

"But I've seen you on the beach," said Ron. "Often."

"I never come down to this end except in the mornings,"
she said. "And I'm hardly ever *on* the beach. I told you."

She dipped her head underwater, and swung her hair back, sleek, from her face.

"Running, in that same blue suit," said Ron. She shook her head, smiling. He followed her out of the water, mystified, but accepting it.

"Well, I guess this is the last time, then," he said. He picked up his glasses and his shirt. "I won't see you on the boardwalk, either."

"On the boardwalk?"

"Where you sit, on that last bench. Maybe you didn't see us. But I thought you did."

"I've never seen you on the boardwalk," she said. "We don't go there much. There's a bunch of us who get together in the evenings. We walk along the sand, play tag in and out of the pilings. You know. But we don't go on the boardwalk. Too noisy and icky." He was silent for a long moment, while she zippered up her jacket and tucked her hair under the white scarf.

"But you did teach us to swim," he said finally. It was almost a question.

"I sure did. My best students." She began to move away, put out a hand and ruffled Joey's hair. "Bye now. See you next year, maybe." Joey looked up grinning.

"Sure thing."

"Yes," said Ron. "Oh, yes. We come here every year." She waved and began to run, and as always they watched her until she was almost invisible in the sunshine and sand.

"Come on, Dad," said Joey. Ron didn't move, but stood staring after the girl.

"Did you think she was the same one?" he asked.

"The same as who?" Ron didn't answer. "There's lots of girls on the beach," said Joey wisely. "They all look a little bit alike. Until you get to know them."

"They do, do they?" Ron smiled down at his son.

"We've got to dry *off*, Dad," said Joey. Ron ruffled his hair as the girl had done.

"Why go back?" he said. "Let's go in the water again."

"Now?" Joey was incredulous.

"Why not? Come on. I'll race you to the Jersey shore!"

"*Okay!*" shrieked Joey, and ran into the water behind his father. Ron didn't look back at him, but began to swim with strong, even strokes. After a while he found Joey at his shoulder, and felt proud that the boy had been able to keep up.

"About time to turn back?" he said. He was beginning to feel a little tired. Joey laughed, naked arms flashing still.

"Not me," he shouted. "I'm going all the way to the Jersey shore." He was a little ahead of Ron now.

"It's an awful long way." Ron smiled. "I guess we'd better go back." But Joey plunged on without answering, and Ron followed, trying to keep the distance between them from lengthening further. Every now and then Joey glanced over his shoulder at his father, grinning with mischievous joy as the wavelets smacked over his head, and Ron grinned back, settling down to a good steady pace now, as they swam on and on into the colder, darker, bluer sea.

Sappho in Wales

ON THE MOUNTAINSIDE, toward the bald and stony summit, was Hilliard's house, with a view of the sea. A quarter of a mile away, along a rough track and a little higher up, was the small and almost unworkable farm that provided her with milk, eggs, a little butter, and a slab of bacon now and then. Occasionally one of the farm girls, either Megan or Olwen, daughters of the dour and taciturn Rees, would come along the track with a couple of chickens in her hand.

When Hilliard first took the house, seven or eight years before, Megan and Olwen were skinny children in skimpy jerseys and serge skirts that showed their bloomers and their dirty knees, scratched and scabbed. They carried the chickens by the scaly yellow feet, and the heads dragged in the dust. Suddenly, just this summer, they had grown up. Olwen bounced along the path in an off-the-shoulder blouse she had bought in Dolgelley, and Megan came dreamily, in sprigged cotton. The chickens dangled clear of the ground, the girls had grown so tall.

Mrs. Rees, their mother, was rarely seen, was only a small bent figure glimpsed between lace curtains in the dark interior of the farmhouse. She seemed to lack the stamina of her fellow countrywomen, had been irrevocably and silently sickly for years, since the birth of Evan, her youngest child. Evan had, in Hilliard's time, grown from a squalling bundle in a dilapidated pram to an undersized, smutty-faced, furtive little boy with his hair all over his eyes. His mornings and evenings were spent avoiding giving a helping hand, to hear Olwen tell it. His days he passed as far as possible from the farm, down in the village with the other boys, fishing in the stream that ran under the road, badgering the bus drivers from Aberystwyth and Dolgelley for pennies, and trying to get chocolate and packets of Woodbines out of the machines on the station platform without putting any money in.

Rees himself plodded off in the mornings on silent farming errands, frowning heavily, carrying a scythe or a rifle, a milk pail or a load of hay. Sometimes he passed the house, giving the barest of nods, wheeling a rusty bicycle, his pockets jingling faintly with small change. He was on his way down to the village, to the stark, slate-colored, and unaccommodating public house, The Green Dragon. It was patronized by none of Hilliard's companions because of the black-lettered sign in the window — DAMN THE ENGLISH.

Olwen had arrived this morning at Hilliard's house, with a couple of chickens.

"They pecked each other to death, look you," she said, lifting up the bloodied heads for them to see. "My Mam thought it best to eat them right away, yes indeed."

"How much?" said Hilliard.

"Five shillings, my Mam says."

"Plain robbery," said Hilliard, placing two half-crowns in

Olwen's hand. "You didn't even have to kill them. And how is your Mam?"

"Getting along, indeed," said Olwen ambiguously. "Getting along. Oh, yes." It might have been in any direction, for better or worse.

"And Evan?"

"That one! The scamp. He collected the eggs this morning, must have been a good dozen, look you, the hens is laying pretty well. But he never brought them to me. He took them down to the village. He will sell them to Roberts the shop, and keep the money. That's the kind he is."

"Do you speak the Cymraeg?" asked Wakefield, hesitantly. He was trying to teach himself Welsh, and carried a book of Welsh poetry with him. He had been at Hilliard's for a week now, and knew one girl from the other. He had meant to save the question for Megan, but somehow it slipped out. At the side of the farmhouse he could see her, hanging out clothes, a small flowered figure moving among the billowing sheets and pillowcases. She did not come to the house as often as her sister. In answer to Wakefield's question, Olwen giggled and nodded, showing the spot of black decay between her two front teeth, blushing furiously, and glancing at Hilliard, who stood at Wakefield's shoulder. She burst into a spate of Welsh, which left Wakefield baffled and laughing. He showed her the book.

"What does this mean?"

"It means . . . It means . . ." She puzzled over the difficulty of translating a poet's tongue into English. "Something about love. It's silly, you see. I shan't tell you!" She glanced again at Hilliard and plucked at the dropped shoulder of her blouse, unused to it yet, making a game of it, instinctively rather than intentionally drawing attention to her smooth brown neck.

"It doesn't matter," said Wakefield sensibly. "There's a translation in the back of the book." He turned away, but Olwen was too pleased at having a conversation with a handsome boy to let him go so quickly.

"Have you seen the ponies?" she said.

"Ponies?"

"The mountain ponies. They've been coming down lately in the early evenings. My Mam says it's to drink at the trough, the weather being so dry, you see. There's no water in the hills. I've seen their hoofprints about the pump. Very small. They must be only about so high." She held her hand out, thigh high.

"*You* haven't seen them, then?" asked Wakefield.

"Only once in my life, when I was a child. I thought they was dogs."

"I've seen them," said Hilliard. "Racing along the ridge, there." Her long forefinger pointed upward.

"You have sharp eyes, then," said Olwen. "Well." She smiled again and almost curtsied. "It is something to look forward to." She left them.

.

Hilliard's house was a perfect summer place. She had made rather a thing of it, in the past several years. The villagers below knew her quite well by now, understood that the group of haversacked students who got out of the train one day early in July was to be directed to Cors-y-Gedyll, where the house stood. The villagers, Roberts the shop, Owens the milk, Hughes and Evans, gossiped about them openly as they clambered off the train, looking them up and down with unfriendly and critical interest, even pointing their fingers so as to make no mistake as to what or whom they were talking about, but speaking in Welsh. It was a little gauntlet to be run through, and Hilliard always warned them.

"They seem unfriendly, but they aren't, not really. It's a peculiar type of Welsh humor, like the sign in the pub window. Partly it's because they're so proud of having a separate language. They like to show it off." Donaldson, with his own view of the ancient peoples, Gaelic and Celtic, wondered if Hilliard was right, wondered if she had really learned anything in all the years she had been coming here.

The students were the more serious of the ones Hilliard taught in winter, at the art school on the outskirts of London. They tended also to be the best-looking, the most fun, the most intense. Summer at Cors-y-Gedyll represented to most of them an accolade, a recognition of their talents. To be invited was a little plume, a medal, and so few were chosen. Rachel, of course, was always there; it was hard to see how the place could have been run without her; but there were never more than two or three others. It was like a little Edinburgh festival, held in high summer, a private celebration, yet something to be witnessed everywhere — in Bromley, Beckenham, Clapham, and Kew — by those who had tried and failed, or those who would never try, but would wish they had.

None of them except Wakefield ever had any trouble climbing up the mountain to Cors-y-Gedyll. They set off, hiking up among the trees, beside the noisy stream, to emerge a mile or so below Hilliard's house, and take the rest of it in great strides, sure of themselves, sure of their welcome. Only Wakefield had trouble, lost his way, took the wrong path, arrived at last with hair curled and ringed with sweat, to sit breathing hard and blue about the mouth in Hilliard's one comfortable chair. He was only eighteen, but it was generally agreed at the art school that he was a probable genius. Donaldson and Rachel agreed to make him comfortable.

.

Donaldson, an adequate painter who could have been more if he had worked harder, forgot his paintbrushes, and spent happy hours experimenting with bits of sheep wool culled from the brambles and tied on twigs. After some consideration he tried human hair, cut in snippets from Rachel's head. He wouldn't have dared touch Hilliard's short blown locks. With an iron-gray eye she defied him to try. But Rachel gave up snippets with pleasure. She was used to being used, and it made her feel of value. She had been an art student for years. She was about twenty-eight, still wearing the dirty, gray flannel shorts of the schoolboy — jeans bound her about her large-boned knees, and she had some idea that shorts were more feminine than trousers — the rough jacket, the sandals, and haversack of the adventurer. She moved from one class to another, never able to decide exactly what her field should be, happily not forced to decide too soon, because her embarrassed industrialist father thought she was mad, and was glad to keep her at a distance from him. She had studied stained glass, giving away what she made, an exquisite composition of the Temptation of St. Anthony, to an impoverished and hideous church in Wandsworth. She had taken up jewelry making, and sold the lot for a song, the rings and bracelets and medallions of topaz and amethyst and chrysoberyl, in order to spend a week in Italy with Hilliard, one Easter. She was wood-carving now, moving it seemed closer to Hilliard, who hacked away at great blocks of stone and marble, and who surrounded the house at Cors-y-Gedyll with horses and angels, chipped out of the coarse granite outcroppings.

"They're nothing," said Hilliard, shrugging. "Just something to do, to keep my hand in. I can't spend the entire summer up here, forcing you people to work, without doing something myself."

"But they're wonderful," said Donaldson. "Don't you realize how you're making history, leaving your mark? Think how they will look, a thousand years from now. The house will be gone, of course, and there will be no one here but a lonely traveler. No one will ever think to come and have a dig in North Wales. Your heads and your horses will still be here, in the wind and the rain and the weather. The lonely traveler will have a guidebook with him. He'll get it all mixed up with the cairns and the cwms and Princes of the Cymru, and wonder what ancient tribal rites were celebrated here. Really, Hilliard, you do have a way of impressing yourself!"

He was teasing her, of course, but she took it well, though Donaldson was the one of them she liked least. She had been taken in by his scholarships, by the impressive grant he had won the year before, by the fact that she had heard him say he would rather cut his throat than teach what he was still unable to do satisfactorily himself. She had a suspicion he had come to Cors-y-Gedyll for fun, out of curiosity, rather than for work. She felt, darkly, there was something significant in his forgetting the tools of his craft. There was that about him that could not be influenced, and she liked people about her on whom her influence flowed, like Wakefield and Rachel. At the art school, Donaldson's humor was refreshing, unpredictable. He seemed sophisticated to the rest of them, as though he were in touch with the world in a way they were not, as though his mind were broad enough to allow him all sorts of attitudes they could not afford themselves. Here at Cors-y-Gedyll there was an edge to his joking, and Hilliard did not like it. She was their leader, they were supposed to be learning something under her direction. But she had to take it well.

.

Wakefield, a shy water colorist with a weak heart he never mentioned but everyone knew about, got up early in the mornings and went off with a bacon sandwich to the mountains, to sketch the moods of the sea, visible from the higher slopes. He was grateful to Hilliard for the opportunity, but not, as the others sometimes were, too grateful to use it. The rest of them, fooling about in the farmyard with scissors and eyebrow tweezers, to collect hair from the goat so as to provide Donaldson with brushes, felt a little resentful toward him.

"What's the matter with *him?*" said Rachel, gesturing to where, beyond the stone walls, below the cairns, Wakefield could be seen, laboriously climbing. She felt like a traitor, saying it, because it was something she could understand quite well. She had often wanted to go off alone, completely alone.

Not the way they did it here at Cors-y-Gedyll, but really.
Really alone. She often thought that next year . . . Some
year, anyway . . .

"He came here to work, and he's working," said Hilliard.
She seemed unperturbed. She straddled the captured goat,
strong brown knees pressing into its sides. "Come on, Donaldson, *clip!*"

Donaldson clipped, and Rachel tugged uselessly on a rope.
Uselessly, because it was clear Hilliard had the goat under
complete control. They laughed and rollicked, and skipped
clear of the goat, and Donaldson had his goat hair, and the
sun beat down on them, but they all felt a slight shadow that
was caused by more than the knowledge that Mrs. Rees was
peering disconsolately at them through the farmhouse window.

"He's probably got a girl over in Harlech," said Donaldson.
It was to ease the tension, and he folded the goat hair into
an old envelope. "Later on, I'll have to get some glue and
fishing twine. You might look for some good straight sticks
for me, Rachel; there's a dear child."

"Why go all the way to Harlech?" said Rachel. "There's
a very pretty girl right here at the farm."

"Olwen?" said Donaldson. "With those teeth?"

"Not her. The other one. Megan."

"An assignation," said Donaldson. "I bet she's ducked
behind the washing and gone haring off up the mountain to
meet Wakefield."

Hilliard frowned slightly. "Perhaps we should have gone
with him," she said. "I don't quite like the idea of his going
off alone, with that heart of his."

"I'll go after him, if you like," said Donaldson, "and catch them in the act. They say people with heart trouble are the same as people with tuberculosis. Passionate." He struck an attitude, a mad artist, about to embrace Rachel.

"Don't be silly," said Rachel. "Megan's at the back of the house, putting sheets through the wringer, and Olwen's helping her. But I'll go, if you want me to, Hilliard. Somebody ought to tell him to take it easy."

Hilliard's arm encircled Rachel's shoulders. "No, not you, Rachel. I suppose nobody need go, really. He'd be furious if he thought we were nursemaiding him." They stood for a moment, looking up at the ridge of the mountain, and then walked back along the track to the house, where Rachel went to churn away at a piece of oak that came off in little curls beneath her lathe, where Donaldson sat down moodily before the door and tried to make a set of brushes, and Hilliard chipped and hammered at the last untouched piece of rock in the garden. It was to be a head of Pan.

"What will you do now, Hilliard?" said Donaldson. "Go to the Hebrides?" She turned, surprised, her lovely Greek head on the magnificent thick brown throat swelling out of the careless blue shirt.

"The Hebrides? What for? I do wish you wouldn't chatter, Donaldson." He lapsed into silence for a while, using glue and tying twine carefully. Rachel, clever Rachel, had found some in a drawer, together with a set of wooden skewers. Hilliard's odd household was rather well equipped with things one wouldn't expect, but he thought she would do well to lay in a collection of artists' supplies. Brushes. Flake white. Turpentine and linseed oil. The sort of things you couldn't possibly do without, and yet so often forgot to carry with you. The basics, the essentials, like milk and butter and eggs, with-

out which you couldn't live but never thought to pack.
Though of course it was his own fault. He should have looked
at the map. She'd said "near Dolgelley." He hadn't realized
Dolgelley was fifteen miles away, and such miles. Up hill and
down dale. Nevertheless . . . He tied a vicious little knot in
the fishing twine, and a few goat hairs got tied in with it. The
damn thing would be like painting with a mop. This whole
business of art was probably a farce. He would have to go into
teaching, after all.

"I mean," he said, "that now you haven't any more rocks.
What will you do? Go up the mountain? Or work on the
Reeses's farmyard?" She stood up, brushing her hands, and
smearing her face with the back of one of them, powdery with
granite dust.

"Perhaps this is the last summer," she said absently. She
stared down at the barely begun head of Pan. The goatish
horns were beginning to show, the fleshy nose, the curl of
hair over the brow. Rachel came out of the house.

"Elevenses," she announced. Elevenses were gin and Bitter
Lemon, drunk out of thick, white china mugs. Afterward,
nobody did much work, but went on to eat lunch, ham and
cheese sandwiches and Eccles cakes bought in the village
below, and have an afternoon nap.

"Isn't Wakefield coming back to lunch?" said Rachel.
"I've made the sandwiches." No one answered her, and she
sat down with them uneasily, at the kitchen table where they
usually drank their gin, glancing often through the window
that faced the long slope to the sea. Wakefield had gone off
in the other direction, up the mountain. She'd never know if
he were on his way back or not.

Behind them were Hilliard's makeshift sleeping arrangements. There was only one bedroom, divided in two by a blanket that hung from a rope strung along the center of the room. On one side Donaldson and Wakefield slept, and Hilliard and Rachel had the other side. There was an occasion when the rope broke, the blanket fell, and the two sexes were revealed in various about-to-go-to-bed attitudes. Rachel and Hilliard shrieked, and clung to one another in panties and brassieres. Wakefield, completely naked, flung himself beneath his sleeping bag, a helter-skelter of white arms and legs. Donaldson, masterful and decent in singlet and shorts, fixed the rope. Hilliard, he noted, had beautiful long muscles in her upper arms and thighs, but no breasts to speak of, while Rachel's, as was almost unpleasantly obvious beneath the loose gray jersey she wore in the daytime, were too large and full for her thin body.

·

Wakefield did not come back for lunch. Hilliard and Rachel retired behind their curtain, and Donaldson thought after all he might try out his brushes. He checked his box, and the easel tied to it, chose a small canvas, and went off up the hill, at an angle to the direction chosen by Wakefield. He found himself a spot where he could look down at the farmhouse, and across at the range of mountains, and set to work. The handmade brushes did, as he expected, handle rather like small floor mops, but there was something interesting in the result. Every now and then he paused, and stood quite still, taking in the day and the weather and the view. Nothing moved but the clouds; even the sea was still. Where do the ponies live? he wondered, dipping his brush, getting out his palette knife. There must be some place where they graze, where they stand and shelter from the sun on the hot afternoons, stamping their feet and flicking their tails to keep off the flies. And so small. He recalled Olwen's hand, held thigh high to indicate their size, and shook his head. Did they really exist? He thought of the tales of the kelpie, in his native Scotland, the immense black water horse that reared out of the lochs to warn of death and doom, the great hoofs scrabbling at the shore, the tossing of the huge head, and the water flying in all directions in storm and thunder. Perhaps the Welsh ponies were just another such story.

After a while, the light changed so that he could not go on, and he packed up his things, wiping rose madder off his brush onto the grass. He had finished, really; he had got what he wanted. There it was. The stone walls of the country mazed across the hillsides, lichened and softened by age and the light, accidentally beautiful, showing the hand of man, patient and lonely. There in the bottom corner was the Reeses's stern little farm, boxlike and uncompromising, a little too tall for its width, and a line of washing and a small figure that was Megan, taking sheets off the line. She had been gone for most of the afternoon, but had appeared suddenly to provide a touch of pink.

He walked back down the hill to the house, and leaned the painting against the wall. Hilliard was chipping away at Pan, but she came over to look at the painting with him.

"It's the best thing you've done," she said. "Wakefield! Rachel! Come and look at this!"

"Do you think so?" said Donaldson. He was doubtful. He had been pleased with himself because he had worked, and turned out something passable, despite the clumsy equipment. That it was the best thing he'd done was unlikely. It was too much like a Van Gogh, for one thing.

"I know so," said Hilliard. "It's your style. It's the way you really see things. These things often happen by accident. It's your way, I can see it. You have an impressionist's eye, Donaldson, and you deny it. You try to tie yourself down to careful, architectural little paintings, and they aren't worthy of you."

"Aren't they?" He was amused, but he was also wounded. Careful, architectural little paintings! It was what he wanted to do, what he found most fun, that planning of shape and size and distance. It was what he had won his scholarships with, and the grants. It was why he loved his studio in Putney, why he had moved into it, to have that splendid view of rooftops and chimneys and skylights. It was why he haunted the Embankment. Not for the river, or the river traffic, not, like some, for the lovers on the benches under the plane trees, but for the contrast of architectural enthusiasm and serenity. But he knew Hilliard's way with artists. She liked to guide them, to direct them into their proper fields; she liked to help. Sometimes, of course, she was right. He looked at the painting, a little troubled. She *was* right. It had come off.

"It's marvelous," said Rachel. "I didn't know you had it in you, Donaldson."

"Didn't you?" he said, piqued.

"It's so . . . It's . . . Oh, I can't express it!" She waved her hands about to show how much she couldn't express it. "It's so *Welsh*. It ought to stay here forever, in Hilliard's house."

"I'd like it," said Hilliard. She looked at the painting seriously, squinting a little. "Would you give it to me, Donaldson?"

"No, I wouldn't," he said. "It goes back with me to Putney, to stand with its face to the wall, and brood on the impossibility of painting with goat's hair."

"I'll buy it, if you like," said Hilliard.

"You won't," said Donaldson, but he felt more troubled than ever. Forty pounds, perhaps? Thirty, anyway, and it would be practically giving it away.

"A nice little painting," said Wakefield. "It has a dash about it. A flair. Who's the little pink blob? Mrs. Rees?"

"That's Megan," said Donaldson.

"Oh, is it?" said Wakefield. He bent forward and examined the painting more closely.

"And what did *you* do today?" asked Donaldson. Wakefield blushed.

"They're in the kitchen," he said. "Just some sketches. Nothing much."

"Just to prove you didn't go to Harlech, and find a girl," said Donaldson. Wakefield blushed harder than ever, and began to get angry.

"Harlech? Of course not. For God's sake, Donaldson, what's the matter with you? You've got girls on the brain."

"Who hasn't?" said Donaldson. "But never mind. I didn't mean it. Let's see the sketches." They went into the kitchen where they were laid out, overlapping on the table.

"No one's seen them yet," said Hilliard. "He only just got back."

"Aha," said Donaldson, but mutedly, looking at the water

colors, and Wakefield's blush subsided. "You must have gone all the way to Dyffryn," said Donaldson. "Isn't that the headland, the point?" Wakefield nodded. They all gazed at the sketches on the table. The sea writhed there, with figures rising out of it. Cloud shapes threatened, turned into angels and held golden trumpets. A silver girl lay naked on the sand. Below the headland, brooding into the sea like a sullen god, were horses, a whole herd of them, galloping, curiously small beneath the rising cliff.

"They're good," said Donaldson. "Is that where the ponies are?"

"Of course, you aren't a painter at all," said Hilliard. "You're a poet."

Wakefield smiled. "What makes you say so?" he asked.

"It's obvious," said Hilliard. "You paint like Blake. You know the awful things he did, muscles and tendons in all the wrong places, men and angels doing the most fearsome gymnastics no one could possibly do without breaking a collarbone or slipping a disk."

"No, Hilliard, I don't paint like that," said Wakefield. He spoke urgently.

"You do," she said. Her long forefinger moved along the drawings. "Look at that. And that. Those shapes are impossible. And they aren't expressionistic, abstract, or anything else. It's just sheer bad drawing. You don't know what you're doing."

"Hilliard, don't you think? . . ." said Rachel.

"No, I don't," said Hilliard. "It's why I'm an art teacher. I *know*. Wakefield doesn't know how to draw."

"But at eighteen . . ." said Donaldson.

Wakefield gave him a furious look. "It isn't a m-m-matter of not knowing how to d-d-draw," he stammered. "I know how to, perfectly well. There's a control that's lacking, I admit that. I make a lot of mistakes. But essentially I think I'm on the right t-t-track."

"You aren't, you know," said Hilliard, smiling. "This isn't your thing at all. You have other talents you haven't expressed yet. You have to find out what they are, before they atrophy and decay, while you're fooling about with something you'll never master. I suggest . . . poetry. You're a poet, Wakefield." She went on smiling, but it was an attack just the same, with something shocking and brutal in it.

Wakefield looked at his sketches in silence, and then gathered them together, rolled them up, and stuck them under his arm. "The thing is," he said, on his way to the door, "I'm a lousy poet, too."

The mist had come down, as it did most evenings. He stood there for a moment at the open door, and then went off, wreathed in it.

"But I was just going to cook supper," said Rachel. "He can't go off like that!" She ran after him, and called, but he was already hidden by the trailing cloud, and he didn't answer.

"Oh, well," said Rachel, hopelessly, hollowly. "It's only chicken stew. I'll save some for him, and warm it up later." She lighted the paraffin lamp, and set it on the table.

"I can smell it," said Hilliard, sniffing. "Basil, rosemary, thyme. What a terrific chef you'd make, Rachel." She turned to Donaldson. "Wouldn't Rachel make a terrific chef?"

"Rachel's very talented," he said. He was still thinking about Wakefield. "Perhaps she should take a course at the

Ritz, and open her own restaurant. Mère Rachelle, chicken stew and dumplings, and stained glass in every window, a semiprecious stone in every roll." He stopped, horrified at himself. He was doing the same thing Hilliard did. "Stick to your lathe, Rachel," he added. "You're doing very well as you are."

"Well, I don't know," said Rachel, seriously. "Cooking is a very creative thing. I *have* sometimes thought . . ." Her voice trailed off, and she messed about with the stew in a bemused fashion.

.

They had just finished eating when Olwen came. She was wearing a shawl over her head and shoulders, damp with mist, picked out in freckles of light from the lamp on the table.

"The ponies are here," she said. "If you will come now, you will see them."

"Now?" said Donaldson.

"They are on their way down," said Olwen. "Evan saw them. He was with the other boys — I gave him a clout for it. He says, you see, they was on the mountain, and they all saw the ponies. They are on their way down, he says."

They followed her along the track, hurriedly and in silence, and stood where she told them to stand, along the stone wall of the farmyard. Olwen went on, arranging the shawl over her shoulders as she went, ducking behind the pigpen out of sight. Three or four miles away, the foghorn sounded, lonely and isolated on the point. They waited. Under the queer white scarf of mist suddenly came the ponies, just two of them, the foal first, the dam after, miniature horses, rough maned but elegant and proud. They skittered about at the gate, and, since it hung on a chain with a good foot to spare, pranced through easily, and went straight to the trough to drink. Afterward the foal seemed inclined to investigate the farmyard, but the mare nudged and blocked him. Intelligently she shoved him toward the only opening there was, the way they had come in. He got away from her, and danced toward the house. With a queer, subdued whinny, she flew between her foal and the buildings. Hilliard moved swiftly. Before Rachel and Donaldson understood what she was doing, she had closed the gate, and twisted the chain twice about the posts, so it no longer hung free. The mare whickered in alarm. The two ponies trotted about the farmyard for a moment, and then with a shrill neigh the mare broke into a canter, and jumped the wall at its lowest point. But the foal was too small, and could not follow. It cantered along the wall, distractedly, while its mother wheeled about on the other side.

"Let it out!" said Donaldson, urgently. "Hilliard, let it out!"

"Hilliard!" said Rachel. But Hilliard hung onto the gate. The foal measured the wall, declining to jump, but hearing its mother's distressed whinnying made up its mind. It leaped, and failed, scrambled, and fell back into the farmyard. Lay there, and did not get up, but kicked and screamed.

"I think it's broken its leg," said Donaldson. Olwen came running. Donaldson pushed Hilliard to one side, and struggled with the chain on the gateposts. They all went and stood beside the fallen pony. On the other side of the wall the mare whinnied again, despairingly, and made off up the hillside.

They heard the *tat-tat* of her hoofs, clicking against the stones and pounding on the turf. Then silence. She had stopped a little way up, was standing there, waiting.

"I'll get my da," said Olwen.

"I thought they might tame it," said Hilliard, conversationally. "It would make a wonderful pet."

Donaldson shrugged. "Rees will have to shoot it now."

The pony kicked in terror, as though it had understood, rolled its eyes and struggled to get up. Its right foreleg was broken, and it collapsed again and again.

Rees came, plodding, carrying a light rifle. He shook his head when he saw the pony, and indicated the gun. "It's all I have, look you," he said. "For rabbits, and such." He gave them a grim, dark, Celtic look, as though he held them responsible. "I'll have to cut its throat."

"Don't you have a mallet, or something?" said Donaldson. "Can't you give it a blow on the head?"

"This is quicker," said Rees. He pulled a short-bladed knife from his belt, knelt down, and cut the pony's throat before their eyes. "A pity, do you see," he said, getting to his feet. He seemed milder. "A wild thing. And the skin? There is hardly enough to make a lady's pocketbook."

They stood there, looking down at the foal, bathed in blood. From a little way up the hillside came the call of the mare, echoed strangely by the foghorn.

"Where is Meganbach?" said Rees. He turned to Olwen. "Have you seen Megan? It is time she came to her supper."

"She is on the mountain, Da," said Olwen. She seemed uneasy, wrapped her shawl more tightly around her. Rees looked defeated, took the pony's hind hoofs in his hand, dragged it bloodily across the farmyard behind him toward the house, and Olwen went with him. The others started back along the track to Hilliard's house.

In the kitchen, the paraffin lamp guttered and flared. There was a black circle on the ceiling above it. Rachel turned down the wick, and went to the bedroom and looked inside.

"Wakefield isn't back yet," she said worriedly.

"He'll turn up," said Donaldson. He brought his painting indoors, propped it against a chair, and stood looking at it. After a while he turned it upside down, sat in another chair, to stare at it for a long time in silence.

Hilliard made herself a gin and Bitter Lemon without consulting the others, and drank it thoughtfully, sitting at the table and clasping the mug as though to draw warmth and reassurance from it. Rachel stacked the supper dishes in the sink and began to pour hot water on them from the kettle. The kitchen filled with steam.

"You don't think he took it badly?" she said.

"Took what badly? Who?" Suddenly Hilliard was in a mood. She tossed off her drink, and flung up her arms. "What are you talking about?"

"Wakefield." Rachel was obstinate. "What we said about his work."

"His work!" Hilliard was scornful. "I'd say it again."

"Of course you would," said Donaldson, without moving his gaze from his painting.

"With that weak heart," said Rachel. "I don't like to see him getting upset."

"He isn't upset," said Hilliard. "He's gone off up the mountain to meet Meganbach." There was a wealth of distaste in her voice.

"Oh, don't be silly," said Rachel.

"You may be right," said Donaldson. "But he's upset, as you put it, just the same."

"He'll have to learn to live with it," said Hilliard, obscurely. And then, "He's debauching that girl. He was with her all afternoon."

They stared at her in surprise. "He couldn't have been," said Rachel, after a long pause, and suddenly, with the triumph of the amateur detective. "Donaldson's got her in his painting. He said so. The little pink blob, isn't that Megan?"

"That was later, then," said Hilliard.

"She was hanging out clothes the entire time," said Donaldson. "God knows why they need so many sheets. Probably Evan wets his bed. He would." It seemed important to lie.

"There you are," said Rachel. She dried her hands on a dish towel, and put her arm around Hilliard's shoulders. "You see?" she said. Hilliard flung the arm violently off.

"I'm going to bed," she said, and went into the other room.

.

After a few hours, Wakefield came back. Blue mouthed, exhausted, and without his sketches. Rachel had joined Hilliard behind the curtain long before. Donaldson gave him some of the chicken stew, and got him to bed, propping a sofa cushion under his shoulders so he could sleep half sitting up. He thought he would take Wakefield back to London with him the next day. None of them was enjoying it. It was pointless to stay. In the morning Megan appeared, with butter in a crock and four brown eggs in her apron pockets. Wakefield was still in an exhausted sleep, but Donaldson thought she was looking for him, the way she cast her eyes about, disappointedly.

"Three shillings," she told Hilliard, and, with a delicacy so pronounced as to seem reluctant, parted with her treasures. She really was a pretty girl, Donaldson noticed, brown and smooth and with great dark eyes, quiet and graceful. The eggs were wrapped separately, each in a sheet of paper. Wakefield's sketches.

"Good lord," said Rachel, recognizing them. "Talk about Carlyle!"

"Who was it," said Donaldson, straightening out the drawings, "whose wife used the pages of his manuscript for jam-jar covers?" He turned to Megan. "He gave them to you?" he said. "Don't you like them?"

Megan went pink, matched her dress. "Oh, yes, indeed, I like them," she said. "But he has a great many, all the same, and he gave them to me. He said he would give me something better, later on." She turned to leave, and Hilliard went with her, talking.

"You think you're in love with Wakefield," she said, in her clear, cold voice. "But you're not, you know." Megan wilted visibly, walking beside her captor, but seemed to protest. "Oh, well," said Hilliard. "All right, you are. But he isn't in love with you."

The rest was lost; they moved out of earshot, down the track. Was Megan crying? Hilliard laid her arm, with its lovely muscles, about Megan's pretty shoulders, and Megan seemed to lean closer to her strong companion as they walked toward the farm.

"Well, that's that," said Donaldson. Rachel was weeping into the sink. "Oh, Lord," he said. "Look, Rachel." He stopped, at a loss.

"It's all right," she said snuffily. "I'm used to it."

"Perhaps you should get unused to it," he suggested.

Rachel turned on him angrily. "Stop pushing me around," she said.

"Perhaps Hilliard had a point," he said cannily. "You are a marvelous cook."

Rachel stopped snuffling. She considered, pondered. "I might make a success of it," she said.

.

Later on that day, Wakefield died, on the station platform. He leaned against the chocolate machine, and slid down it quietly. So quietly that Donaldson, standing beside him, waiting for the train, did not notice. A small, white-faced boy with hair all over his eyes — Evan, probably — shouted. The porter came running, and there was Wakefield, lying on the ground, pillowed awkwardly on his haversack. An ambulance came, and he was taken to the hospital in Dolgelley, but it was at least twenty minutes too late.

Donaldson, unable to leave as he had planned, took the haversack back to Cors-y-Gedyll. In case there should be something in it distressing to Wakefield's parents, he went through the contents, and found a sheaf of poems addressed to Megan.

"I suppose I ought to destroy these," he said, looking around the kitchen table.

Rachel burst into noisy sobs, and got up to stir a panful of meat and herbs.

"Do as you like," said Hilliard, shrugging into a mugful of gin and Bitter Lemon. "I said he was a poet. But the truth is, Wakefield had no artistic sense."

Girl Bathing

IT COULD BE ANYWHERE, any time, a scene of water meadows, a stand of spindly trees, a stream, and a girl kneeling in the shallow water, looking pensively down at a weed, a pebble, or perhaps at her own blurred reflection. It must be early in the year, the trees are bare branched. There are no shadows, and the water must run cold. Yet she kneels there, the water nymph, naked and contemplative. The way her hair is done, cut quite short and fashionably, is all that gives the game away. She is not a nymph after all, but a real girl, and this is a photograph pasted in an album, with the name inked in beneath. EDITH, 1946. Winderham took this, the neat capitals proclaim, with Quentin's camera.

The photograph album is spread open on the floor of the little room that opens onto the balcony and the steps down to the garden. Brilliant sunshine streams through the glass-paned door, illuminating the pages, the dust motes in the air, the rows of books on the shelves, and the fair head of Nina, Edith's daughter, bent over the old photographs.

A Sunday afternoon cocktail party is going on in the next room. The name Edith is spoken often, flashes gaily, a bird flying from the mouth of one speaker to the next, as Edith herself moves rapidly and colorfully among her guests. She is wearing a silk dress today, with pink and green flowers on it. No sign here of the nymph. Those years are gone.

"Edith, what a genius you are. No one else gives such good parties." "Edith, where do you find your clothes? Such a gorgeous silk." "Edith, I brought a friend, I hope you don't mind. When I told him about you he simply insisted — "

And then Quentin's voice. "Edith, Winderham's here."

The girl looking at the photographs had opened the door to him a few minutes before. Winderham. There he was, up from the country, exhausted, white faced beneath grime, a bristled jaw and red scratches that indicated he had shaved recently, but not recently enough. Leaning against the lintel as though he were almost too tired to stand upright, coughing as usual, and worse than she remembered.

"Is Edith at home?" He groped for the rest of Edith's name, found it. "Mrs. Forrester?" He'd forgotten Nina, Nina thought. Of course she must have grown, changed, since his last visit. When was it, a year ago, something less, a little more? She was, to him, just any young girl, seventeen, eighteen years old, who opened the door when he knocked. She might even be the maid, careless on a Sunday, her uniforms out to the laundry.

"Of course," said Nina. He brought so much with him, some of the happiest, the strangest, most significant moments of her childhood. The first teddy bear, a box of marbles — had he really understood she was a girl? — a wooden puppet carved in Russia, a brooch in the shape of a basket of flowers — of course, he must have. And, of course, the photograph.

He was the other half of a puzzle. She led him through the hall, and flung open the door of the party room for him. "She's expecting you," she said, wickedly, into the immediate din, shut the door behind him, went into the room next door and began hunting through the photograph albums for the ones she wanted.

And now, on the heels of Quentin's warning, Edith saying: "Winderham, how lovely to see you!" Light chatter, and then Winderham, deep and hoarse, cutting across it.

"Edith, could you lend me five pounds?"

.

Nina got to her feet, and opening the glass-paned door went outside onto the balcony. She found Winderham's plea distressing, though it was nothing new. And of course Edith had not expected him. He had not even been invited. He was never invited. He moved so often, and lived in such obscure places that no invitation could ever reach him in time, even if Edith had thought of it. And yet, by some unerring instinct, he always turned up at Edith's parties — or perhaps it was that she gave parties so frequently Winderham could hardly fail to arrive when one was being given. Unsuitably dressed, unsuitably, that is, for the occasion, but perfectly suitably for himself, shabby and stained, hair too long and trousers too short, dirt beneath his fingernails and wearing workman's boots with broken laces, he waited impatiently for the moment when he could confront Edith, speak privately with Edith. How could he do it, Nina wondered, set out like that, journey for such distances, hitchhiking on the backs of trucks, riding pillion behind motorcyclists, sleeping in barns and henhouses, never knowing what he would find when he got there? To Edith's house. They might have gone away, left for the summer, flown to another country. They did these things, and it was amazing to Nina that Winderham never picked those times to come. At least, she had assumed he didn't, and suddenly felt a cold clutch at the heart, as she imagined that he might have, easily could have — it was the first time she had ever thought of such a possibility — and found no one at home.

Some of Edith's friends, the new ones, would be surprised to see Winderham there, wonder where he belonged in the hierarchy, think him an old hanger-on, probably a relative. A scapegrace brother of Edith's perhaps, a sponging cousin. Others, the ones who dated from the same period as Winderham, would be not at all surprised, take for granted his dirty impatient presence, ask him gracefully where he was living now, and if he was doing much work. Some of them, too, vanished from time to time, tried living on the coast of Spain, a Greek island, or — last year it had been quite the thing — far north, in a Norwegian hamlet. They always turned up again, as Winderham did, and assumed he did the same as they, struggled to recapture an errant muse, came back with little to show for time and money spent but happy recollection and some interesting bits of folk art, embroidery, and pots, or, in the case of some who had gone to Lapland one summer, a pair of reindeer antlers. Somewhere in their luggage a poem, the first notes for a new book, a thin folio of sketches to be worked up at a later date.

Winderham didn't speak much, hardly answered their questions, and then in a preoccupied and absent manner, looking about the room for Edith. Quentin would join him, sit beside him, give him a drink, watch imperturbably as Winderham, handling the stemmed glass clumsily, splashed a few drops of the drink on Edith's green satin sofa. Quentin would call Winderham's attention to it, but insist that it didn't matter, in that easy bluff way he had that hid a hard core of something — but what? Nina wondered. What? Easy and bluff, that was Quentin, and Nina wondered now, standing on the balcony overlooking the garden, how her father could be like that, considering the photograph in the album. What did it all mean? What had happened? What had happened then, and what was going on now?

She knew her curiosity, somehow so urgent in recent months, she couldn't think why, was — just a little — morbid. Salacious even, and she was ashamed of it, though she could think of no one among her contemporaries who would not be considerably more titillated than she at the sight of any mother of theirs, or, for that matter, a mother of anyone else's, kneeling in a stream like that; breasts, belly and flanks bare, on a cool gray morning in 1946 or any other year. Encouraged to love the good, the true, the beautiful, and to despise vulgarity as though it were a religion practiced by pagans, she kept her inquisitiveness secret, though privately believing the good, the true, and the beautiful somewhat lacking in savor.

"That was taken near Norwich," Edith had said recently of a group photograph of variously and amusingly hatted persons standing in a wet-looking field. "The one in the middle is me. Good lord, how hideously we used to get ourselves up." This was on one of the few occasions when she had time to talk to Nina, an afternoon when something else had fallen through, a luncheon party canceled, a gallery opening show so dull that Edith had come home early. She turned the page, came upon the photograph of herself in the stream. Nina waited for revelation, but none came. "Winderham was living in an old mill, then. We all went down and stayed with him. Took our own food and drink, of course. Winderham never had anything. Always as poor as a church mouse. Dedicated to his art, poor darling." She sighed, brushed her fingers over the photograph to remove specks of dust which must, it seemed, since they remained where they were, have been in the lens of the camera. "But we had good times. What a Bohemian lot we were. Champagne, potted shrimp. None of us could afford it really, but everyone had something. Quentin had a little jar of truffles in his raincoat pocket. Winderham shot a hare, and we cooked it. Quentin skinned it first, and he said he'd make me a pair of fur gloves, but he never did." And a tiny piece of the puzzle fell into place. When Quentin gave Edith the fur coat, last Christmas, he'd said, "Instead of gloves," and they had laughed at her mystification.

"It didn't taste very nice," said Edith. "One of the girls, Pamela something, broke a tooth on a bullet. Quentin took a picture, it ought to be here somewhere, of Winderham holding up the hare, with a rifle in his hand. Sort of African. You know, like a lion." She flicked through the pages, but couldn't find the photograph. "Quentin had a Leica — he liberated it in Germany — with a telescopic lens. Winderham was mad about it. They both were, and took masses of pictures. Everyone said he ought to give up what he was doing, and take up photography."

"Who, Quentin?" said Nina.

"No, Winderham."

"Were you engaged, then?" said Nina.

"Quentin and I? Oh dear, no. In our crowd you didn't get engaged. We laughed at engagements. You just got married, or didn't get married. But we did some mad things." She closed the album. "Of course, everyone thought we would get married," she said.

"You and Quentin?" said Nina.

"No, no. Winderham and I."

Nina walked down the steps into the garden. Of course there wouldn't be any trouble about the five pounds. Even in the lean days ("Don't you realize water costs money? When will you learn to turn off the bathroom taps properly?" "For heaven's sake, Nina, are you trying to burn up all the profits?" Quentin, switching off her bedside lamp, shining under the door at midnight) Edith had managed to scrape up two or three out of the housekeeping money; Quentin had turned out his pockets, contributed half a crown, or a ten-shilling note. Now Edith would probably offer Winderham ten, even fifteen, be refused. "Well, I can't break it. It's either take it or leave it." And Winderham would take it. Then he would sit about until the last guests had gone, lost in a dream, giving in to his tiredness, watching the great cherry tree outside the windows as it slowly shed its petals, and be hustled down to the kitchen to be fed by Edith ("So much fun, when there's only a few of us left!") with filling foods, egg sandwiches and slices of ham, pickled walnuts and slabs of cold meat, while Quentin, suddenly remembering, would dash upstairs with a dishcloth soaked in cold water, to sponge away at the drops of gin Winderham had spilled on the sofa.

"I really must be going," Winderham would say suddenly, starting up, though his plate, still laden, lay before him on the table, and no matter what they said or how they implored, he would leave, and go off down the front steps and vanish into the street, on his long walk back to wherever he had come from, or, perhaps, to a new place he hadn't said anything about. Sometimes, though, he did stay the night, borrowing Quentin's razor and sometimes a clean shirt or a pair of socks, going away early in the morning, leaving behind a mess of coffee cup and saucer, sugar, grains of coffee, spilled milk on the table, and a piece of burnt toast in the sink, mute evidence of his inability to manage by himself.

"He can't go *on* like this!" Edith would exclaim. It was hard to know exactly what she meant. Living alone, his gypsy life, cooking sordid messes in tin cans — or leaving Edith's house in such disorder.

"He does, though, doesn't he?" said Quentin pleasantly.

.

A vine was trained against the garden wall. In a good summer it bore grapes — they were darkening now, tight spider-ridden bunches of them, bitter green in spring, and Edith made wine in September, insisting that Nina and Quentin join her in the ceremony. They stood, uncomfortably close, barefooted, in a large but not quite large enough wooden tub, feeling the grapes as nodules under their feet, waiting for Edith to signal them, which she did by singing the first part of an old Tuscan song. They were supposed to recognize it and be ravished, did and were, singing their parts with enthusiasm as they stamped up and down. Their feet were stained by the grape skins long after the wine was made. Nina in the autumn, barefoot at a picnic, looked down at her purple feet when someone — a stupid fat girl — asked her, "Is that a birth defect?" New language for something hideous and handicapping. She shrugged. "You could call it that." Not for anything would she admit she had been treading grapes, would rather claim an abnormality of her own, something in her skin, a port-wine mark as it was called. But on *both* feet? The fat girl said, with interest, "It runs in your family, doesn't it?" And looking at her mother and father, Nina saw their feet were as deeply stained as her own. "The curse of the Forresters," she said, and lay down in the cool sunlight, forbidding further conversation.

Wine from the previous year was drunk on Guy Fawkes night. The devil's feast night, Edith called it, harking back to an earlier time than the seventeenth century, flinging off the woolen shawl she wore throughout the winter. A saturnalia. She and Quentin and their guests danced about in front of the bonfire built dangerously close to the winter-dead cherry tree. Nina and any current boy friend — David, last year — sat and watched them, sitting on a damp log considered not fit for the saturnalian service, listlessly drank their wine, and refused to taste Edith's special gingerbread concoction. Both dieting, they said.

Though it was a shame to disappoint Edith like that, Nina thought guiltily. She took such pleasure in being arty and batty, Bohemian, gypsyish, thoroughly unsound. She was so contradictory, her drawing room hung with modern art and crystal chandeliers, a Persian rug on the floor, silver goblets to drink out of, everything cost such a lot. And yet, treading her own grapes, and occasionally weaving the material for a new skirt, dying a pair of curtains for a neglected downstairs room. Just the same, as the catherine wheel spun, Nina and her boy friend — David, last year — sat glumly on their log, and, in fact, bored, swiveled around and turned their backs on the display, ignored the rockets and the sparklers, and the boy friend strummed tunelessly on his guitar. It was a part of him really, attached to him by a strap around his neck, as though it had grown there.

"I say," said someone, "do you play?" Visualizing the night turned Mexican, Guadalajara, the clapping of hands, and drinking — something more potent than Edith's wine perhaps — and a wild stamping of feet.

"A few chords." The boy friend shrugged, disowning the guitar, as far as its music went.

"Oh? Well, let me try. I know a few things. 'Home on the Range.' You know. Western stuff." Reached out his hand for the guitar, and the boy friend reared away.

"Uh-uh. Borrow someone else's guitar. Not this one."

"But if you don't play it — "

"What difference does that make? It's still mine." And the boy friend sat, closely pressed against Nina, protective arm around the silent instrument.

.

Today, this Sunday afternoon, she walked into the garden, small and rectangular, but somehow boundless. The enormous cherry tree, blossoming like a cloud in the warm days of May, almost over now, petals falling faintly, drifting to the ground like warm and languid snow.

"Not another tree like it, outside of Kew Gardens," said Quentin proudly, every year.

"Awful," said Winderham, squinting at it through the window. "Shapeless. It looks like a bloody feather bed. Nothing you can do with that."

.

Nina leaned over the garden wall, looked down into the garage below.

"Hullo, David," she said. The young man with the chamois in his hand looked up quickly, then down again, continued polishing the headlights of the car. "There's a party going on in my house," said Nina.

"Mmm. I saw the cars. Fun?"

"Not very. The usual. Winderham's there." She sighed.

"Winderham. You told me about him before. The one who married the Indian girl, and abandoned her in Rome."

"That's Castellon. No, you remember. *Winderham.*" But he was obstinate.

"You have such peculiar friends."

"Not me. My parents. Can I come down?"

"If you like." He abandoned his polishing, held out an arm and she jumped down, staggered a little, and recovered herself against his shoulder.

"Damn." She examined her stockings.

"Shouldn't go mountain climbing in nylons," he said, and picked up his cloth again. "Winderham. Lives in a shepherd's hut in the Pennines."

"Right. Only that was last year. I think he's down in Dorset now." She was leaning decoratively against the big double doors of the garage, one leg crossed over the other, arms folded. He threw her a tin of polish suddenly, almost viciously.

"Since you're here —" She started, caught it, almost fell.

"Oh, all right. Got another rag?" He jerked his head toward a heap of them, on the garage floor. Humbly, she picked one up, smeared it with polish, and started on the car door opposite him. "He looks worse than ever," she said. "Probably he's tubercular."

"Who?"

"Winderham."

"Tubercular," scoffed David jealously. "Just the sort of thing he would have."

"How do you know? You've never met him," said Nina.

"I know a lot about your friends," he told her. "Those people you're always talking about. The one with the emerald earrings, who sat for all those movie stills and didn't make it. The intense one."

"Veronica!" Nina burst out laughing. "I can't stand her. She has those huge square white teeth."

"Castellon. You had quite a crush on him."

"Oh, David, he's old. He has a bald head."

"You didn't like it when he got off with the Indian girl," David said shrewdly. "You thought he was very amusing, when he told about how he left her sitting at the café in the Via Veneto, and went off to catch a plane back to London. What a sod." He polished furiously, while Nina slowed down, after a fast beginning.

"Who else?" she said, looking at him over the top of the car.

"Winderham," he said. "Winderham. Always Winderham." And then, quickly, without waiting for her reply, "If you don't get on faster than that, we won't be able to go for a spin afterward."

.

They went to the river in the little red car, drew up at the edge of a field of golden mallows, swampy and treacherous, watched two swans preening themselves on the bank.

"We could swim," said Nina. But David was quarrelsome and moody, lit a cigarette, spitefully tossed the match out of the window without offering her one. She noticed that his sweater was handmade, beautifully cable-stitched, oatmeal colored.

"I want to take some photographs," he said, touching the camera on the seat between them.

"Feelthy pictures?" said Nina, almost hopefully.

"Just ordinary pictures."

"All right. When? Now?" She was eager.

"When we're ready." He puffed at the cigarette, and she folded her arms, stared resentfully at the swans, who now, with a large flapping of wings, approached the water, took to it with some plunging, appeared gracefully, perfect forms, floating in their proper element.

"It's a funny thing about swans — " she began.

"Okay, ready for the action?" said David. They spoke at the same time, laughed, and as he took the camera out of its case she leaped joyously out of the car, stood in the slight breeze and stretched her arms.

"Stand over there," he directed, and she took her place

under a willow, looking out from beneath the green fronds. "Did you notice the swans?" he asked her, as he fiddled with the camera. "A funny thing about swans, they always look so — "

"Oh, David." She sighed, and he clicked the shutter.

"Splendid. Okay, another one. Look over there." He took a great many photographs of her, posed in this way and that, and the swans swam downstream and were gone.

After the picture taking, they lay under the willow, chewed blades of grass and talked, the camera between them. He had a good thing going, David told her, with the firm he was working for. The boss's son was pulling out, turning to something different, going to Australia probably.

"I'm something of the white-haired boy, now," said David, and kissed her lightly, celebrating this positive turn in his affairs. He didn't ask her to marry him, nothing like that, but Nina thought in time he would.

As the day wore on, they left the river and drove back toward town. David drew in abruptly, dangerously, with a spurt of gravel, at a roadhouse on the way.

"Might as well have a drink," he said. "Want something to eat?" She nodded, and they went inside to a brilliant bar, scarlet and chrome, music playing, a good many people sitting around. "Oh God, the camera," said David, and went back to the car for it. The roadhouse, called whimsically The Sticky Mesh, was such a change from the river and the field of mallows that Nina felt out of place and uncomfortable, as though she had weeds in her hair, and pinions in place of arms. Several men turned and looked at her, leered, she thought, before turning away again as the swing door opened and David came back in.

"It could have been stolen," he said, placing the camera carefully beside him on the red plastic-covered seat. "Now." He clapped his hands slightly together. "Beer? Or something stronger? Sandwiches? Beef, ham? Pickles, the lot?"

"Oh, yes," said Nina.

"Well, but which?" said David. She thought.

"Gin," she said. "One of those orange drinks."

"An orange blossom? Okay."

"Ham and cheese," she said, in a rush. "And pickles."

"The pickles go with the beef. Never mind, I expect you can get them." He went to the bar, gave the order, very masculine and efficient, in the beautiful sweater, jingling change in his pocket. "One orange blossom. One pale ale. Ham and cheese, pickles, and one ham only."

The room went darker as she slowly sipped and even more slowly chewed, the music was as loud, but somehow she found she could hear David better, as he went on about his job and his prospects.

"Come on," he said at length. "You've had three of those, and you've only eaten half your sandwich."

"I don't seem to be very hungry," she said, contrite. "I'm sorry. It's been such a glorious afternoon."

"All that fresh air," he agreed. "But we'd better be getting back." She must have gone to sleep in the car, for suddenly they were there, and she was at the front door, waving good-bye to David as he roared in reverse to the garage. She'd forgotten her key, and knocked gently. Were they asleep?

To her surprise, Winderham opened the door.

"They've gone to bed," he said. "Edith and Quentin. I think the party was a bit much for them. I'm staying the night." He led the way, quite as if he knew it, into the kitchen downstairs. "She did say," he told Nina, getting out bread and cheese in an accustomed manner, "she thought you might have put in an appearance."

"I did," said Nina, defensive. "I was here for hours. Anyway, it wasn't my party."

"Oh, no. It was Edith's party." He coughed a little, then a lot, and she handed him some paper tissues from the sideboard. "Yes." He spat, delicately, into the tissues. "It was Edith's party. But *you* had a good time, I can tell. You look — You're glowing."

"Am I?" said Nina, pleased, a little embarrassed. "I've already had something to eat." He was handing her a plate, a paper napkin.

"Oh, where?"

"A place called The Sticky Mesh."

"Are you sure you're saying that right?"

"The Sticky Mesh? Yes, it is rather clever, isn't it?"

"Well, a little more can't hurt," said Winderham, putting food on her plate. And suddenly she was ravenously hungry, could hardly wait for him to cut himself a wedge of cheese before starting in on her own. "I hate to eat alone."

"But you always do," said Nina. "Don't you live alone?"

"Ever since I gave up my studio." He looked a little wolfish, biting down hard into a crust.

Nina had been to his studio once. In the days before he became a wanderer. Edith had taken her. It was winter, and she and Nina both wore little fur hats and carried muffs. Dimly, now, Nina perceived that they had been quite smartly dressed, and that somewhere in the background was a woman who was not. Something of a slattern in fact, a dirty blouse and her sleeves rolled up to her elbows, a lot of untidy dark hair. Her name was Margaret. There was a quarrel in the kitchen, something bitterly denunciatory said, a door slammed and a plate smashed. It was suggested that Nina go out into the garden for a while, and though she would rather have stayed with her mother, breathing in the scent of oil and acid, meddling happily with the metal plates Winderham used for his etchings, and been served tea on a tray — this was evidently being prepared, to Winderham's orders, during the quarrel — she was taken by the hand, put outside, and told to play. Play what? She looked about her and found herself alone in a narrow weedy rectangle, surrounded by the high whitewashed walls of other buildings. It was like being in a box with the lid off, the sky visible, but no hope of ever climbing out. She walked about for a few minutes, cold, with her hands tucked into the little fur muff, the replica of the one her mother wore. In one corner someone had planted a clump of daffodils. They stood, not fully grown out of the ground, buds not yet visible, straight green leaves, a forlorn promise of spring. At the foot of one of the walls a curious fungus grew, crinkled half circles of enormous size. She kicked one of them, and it broke softly away, and when she mashed it savagely under her heel the mess was as though she had killed something.

"You can come in now, poor baby," said Winderham, and suddenly she was inside again, and tea was indeed served on a tray, and mixed biscuits laid out on a plate.

.

"It's cold down here," she said now to Winderham, as they finished eating. "Why don't we go up and sit in the little room? I'll make some coffee."

"I'm taking a drink," said Winderham. "I don't often get it. How about you? Or are you allowed?"

"Of course I'm allowed." She was indignant.

"Well then." He poured from a bottle into two glasses, and carried both drinks upstairs. Carefully Nina turned out the kitchen light, and they stumbled up in the dark. The little room was cosy, lighted by only the fire and a small lamp in a corner by the bookshelves. They sat and drank in silence for a while, Winderham coughing occasionally, and quite suddenly he came over to her and sat on the arm of her chair. Why, he's going to make love to me, thought Nina, and leaning over on the other side, set her drink carefully on the floor. She let him kiss her, responded dreamily, but jerked away when she felt his fingers inside her blouse.

"No, no. Winderham, please, no." He was lying half on top of her, and she stared up at him in the moment before he moved. Red flames flickered on his forehead and his nose, dark shadows at his eyes. Handsome, gypsyish, craggy, and lean. And then he sat upright, shook his head, drank from his glass.

"I'm sorry," he said. "I'm old enough to know better. That's the sort of thing you ought to get over at eighteen."

"I'm sorry too," said Nina nervously. "But I *am* eighteen; what are you supposed to get over?"

"You're very like Edith."

"Like Edith?" She felt the deepest of pain, and a strange excitement. "Were you in love with Edith, then?"

"In love with Edith?" He gave a mingled laugh and cough. "No. Not really." He took a package of cigarettes out of the pocket of his jacket, hanging over the back of a chair.

"And me?" She meant, Are you in love with me?

"I'm old enough to be your father," he said.

"Perhaps you are," she said. If she had hoped to shock him, there was no sign of it. He inhaled cigarette smoke, coughed again.

"Not the remotest possibility. And I'm glad of it." She was about, passionately, to agree, pushing herself forward in the armchair, when something in his tone halted her.

"Why not?"

"I shouldn't like to have fathered you. I shouldn't like the responsibility." The conversation had taken an unexpected tack, but she was prepared to pursue it.

"So Quentin is my real father?"

"It's a wise child, et cetera, et cetera. No. I didn't mean that." He shook ash into the fireplace. "You won't be Quentin's very long. Some nice young —"

"Some nice young man will come along and sweep me off my feet and give me lots of lovely babies to take my mind off," said Nina. "Which is just exactly the very thing I don't happen to want."

"Ah, well. You will, in time," said Winderham equably. He leaned against the mantel, and she thought of warning him that his trousers might scorch if he didn't move away. "At that, though, you may be right." He moved suddenly, slapping at his calves. "Extra babies aren't exactly in high demand in the world, just now."

"Ah, Winderham."

"Don't cry." He laughed a little. "I said that exactly as if you *were* my daughter."

"I don't want to be your daughter." She sniffled deeply,

into the arm of the chair. "I'd like — I mean — Why couldn't I go with you? *Be* with you?"

"Be with me? Dear girl, I'm an old married man."

"You've got a wife?"

"Had her for years," said Winderham. The angry woman at the studio, that time.

"Margaret? Marjorie? Something like that?"

"Margaret, yes. How did you know? Has Edith ever — ?"

"I just remembered it," said Nina. "I was there, once. And Edith never — Children?" There was a pause.

"None."

"You practice what you preach," said Nina sadly.

"Not intentionally. We don't live together. But we've never divorced. She saves me from all kinds of difficulties. But not money ones." He shook the glass in his hand so the melting ice tinkled against the sides, looked deeply into it. "No. Not money ones."

"Female ones," said Nina, feeling marvelously perspicacious. He gave a half-strangled laugh and nodded.

"It's getting very late," he said. "I must be — Well, do you know, I think I won't spend the night. I'll just be off."

"Walk in the dark?" said Nina. She was on her feet too, making the motions of fixing her hair, smoothing it down into wings on either side of her face.

"Why not? I'm a fast walker, you know. I'll be there, sometime tomorrow."

"Where is there?" said Nina. He hesitated.

"I don't know. West, perhaps. There's a place I've heard of — " He gave her an odd look, placed his glass on the mantel, shrugged on his shabby jacket. "I don't suppose — "

he began. "I mean, I don't like to ask, but — Nina — " (Ah, she had a name!) "could you lend me some money? Not much. About five pounds?"

And of course she was up in her bedroom, turning out her handbag, counting out what she had. It came to two pounds twelve shillings. A few extra coppers made it look worse, and she put them back, zippered up the purse.

"It's all I've got," she told him. "Didn't Edith — ?"

"I hated to ask them," he said. "They seemed to be a bit short. Sunday, of course, banks all shut. But I'll manage."

They went to the front door, silently, and Nina opened it. A few cars went by, moonlight shone on the steps.

"Well, I'll be off." He made a cavalier gesture. "Coming with me?"

"Off with the raggle taggle gypsies O?" She shook her head. "After all, no. Thanks anyway, Winderham."

"No goosefeather bed, I agree." He pinched her cheek. "You're a very bourgeois little girl, did you know that? They've brought you up very well." She looked at him, standing in the doorway like a ghost.

"*Am* I your daughter?" she managed finally.

"God, no," he said. "What a circle that would make!"

"Good-bye, then."

"Good-bye." He left; and with enormous regret, knowing that the next time he came she would be completely different, gone, married perhaps, flown to another country, never lend him money again, she closed the door, just catching a picture of him at the bottom of the steps, turning and raising his hand in a kind of salute.

Briholme in Winter

A LONG TIME AFTERWARD they found themselves staying at the hotel where they had spent their honeymoon, and at the same time of year, in the dead days between Christmas and New Year's Day. An odd time for a wedding, as Harriet and Robert were always the first to admit, when all the pretty, glittering things were put away, and there was nothing much left of celebration but the chemists' shop windows, laced with colored paper streamers; artfully half-spilled boxes of confetti standing among the hot-water bottles and the displays of Evening in Paris.

Briholme had not changed at all. And neither have I, thought Harriet, overcome by depression and dismay as they drove up to the hotel, even though she had chosen to stay there, as she had chosen it for their honeymoon. Made, in fact, the same deliberate mistake. The bored doorman, like the other — the original — bored doorman, tucked his chewing gum behind the triangular scales of the palm tree before he opened the door of the car. The fact that it was a Daimler made no impression on him, but he brightened at the sight of Harriet's emerald-green leather coat, and promised to have the car put away in the garage behind the hotel.

There was a wheelchair in the lobby, and several pairs of crutches stood in a sort of umbrella stand. Through the double doors of the lounge, decorated in a thin, halfhearted fashion with four blue paper streamers that curled from the overhead lighting fixture to the four corners of the room, Harriet could see the old ladies, moving about a little restlessly because it was close to dinner time, picking up magazines and putting them down again, showing one another knitting patterns, and gossiping with what she vividly remembered to be clicking teeth and a tiny drool in the corner of the mouth. Every now and then one of them cast her eyes skyward in an odd manner that Harriet knew meant she was looking at the clock on her side of the doorway.

"Do I have time to bathe before dinner?" she asked her husband. He had just finished signing the register.

"Dinner's at seven o'clock," he said, in the hushed and respectful voice suitable to the hotel. "It's five to, now." They followed a wizened "boy" up the carpeted stairs, and along a carpeted corridor. There was no elevator at the Palm Gardens Hotel.

"And not a single other place in the town," said Harriet. "You'd think, after all these years . . . But no. Just the same as it was."

"I asked," said Robert. "She said The Copper Kettle serves a very nice *tea*. Scones, sardines on toast. You know. But it closes at five-thirty. There's a sort of snack bar at the station. Ham sandwiches and cake, from eleven to one. And there's a coffee bar on the Esplanade, but it's closed from September to May."

"That's an improvement," said Harriet. "In our day there wasn't anything at all on the Esplanade, except cripples, wrapped in red hospital blankets. Anything else?"

"Nothing at all," said Robert.

"Stone dead," said Harriet. "But never mind. I'll just wash my face and hands. And maybe we could go for a walk, after dinner."

"Perhaps there's a pub somewhere about," said Robert, but not as though he believed there would be.

"I think Briholme's the only town in England without one," said Harriet, and he nodded.

"We couldn't find one before, I do remember that." He tipped the "boy," and closed the door of their room. Harriet opened her suitcase, and placed her hairbrush, hand mirror, and a bottle of cologne on the dressing table. The hairbrush and mirror were backed with silver, a little heavy and old-fashioned, dented in places. They had been a present from her mother, another of the heavy and old-fashioned things she had been given when she married, and Harriet remembered how proud of them she had been, the first time she put them down on the dressing table in this hotel. They had seemed to give a solidity, a permanence, to her marriage that so far, only a few hours old, it lacked. And never, thought Harriet, with a slight sense of shock, quite gained. That had been, though, in quite another room, down another passage, up another flight of stairs.

It had taken them a long time to get over having made such a mistake — fancy spending your honeymoon in a hotel for retired and decrepit old ladies — but in recent years they had made rather a good story out of it. One on which they could, as people said, dine out; one that was greeted with appreciative laughter at cocktail parties.

"We just didn't know where to go," Harriet would explain, glancing at Robert. "There were so many places you *couldn't* go to, because of the war."

"Barbed wire all over the east coast," said Robert. "And London was impossible, with the air raids. Otherwise I think we would have just gone to the Dorchester, and had breakfast in bed for fourteen days."

"It's what we should have done," said Harriet. "There wasn't a single air raid in the two or three weeks after we got married. But we had romantic ideas. We wanted somewhere on the coast, and quiet. Devonshire cream. A farmer's wife who had bottled her own blackberries. Roast goose. Apples and raisins. Extra bacon, that wasn't from the black market."

"We must have been mad," said Robert gloomily.

"So finally," said Harriet, "I simply stuck a pencil into a map of the southwest of England. Briholme."

"We'd never heard of it before," said Robert. "And neither had anyone else. So we went there."

"It did sound awfully romantic," said Harriet. She was still excusing herself. Sometimes at this point she would feel a little sad, but always glanced around comically at her friends, and asked, "Doesn't it sound romantic? Briholme. Sort of Danish. A little village all alone and lost, a wild place on the cliffs, with lots of secret little coves."

"Well, it wasn't like that at all," said Robert. "I had an inkling, but Harriet insisted." Exchanging the merest grimace, they went on to tell what Briholme was like. The red-brick villas, called Upalong and Downalong, and Bide-a-Wee, and Dhu-Cumin. The awful hotel. Sometimes, when they described the old ladies and the cripples, the shoe shop that sold only high-buttoned boots, and the row of nursing homes along the cliffs, the laughter got so loud they found they were missing out really good bits. Like the knitting patterns, and the old girl who thought there was a mouse in her shoebag, and the time Harriet was cornered in the lounge and advised to use a vinegar douche if she wanted a really healthy baby.

What they never mentioned was the house on the beach.

·

Harriet, staring at her dressing-table set, was acutely conscious of Robert, busily filling the porcelain washbasin in the corner with water, unwrapping a cake of hotel soap. He washed his hands, and mopped at his face with a corner of a linen towel, dipped in warm water.

"I don't think I need to shave," he said.

"No," agreed Harriet. What had become of the lean and spare young man he had been? What had become of the poet, the bridegroom, the man who hated things to be just so? He weighed himself on the bathroom scales every morning, the daily ritual of observing his weight gradually increase somehow making up for his refusal to diet. But somewhere inside him existed still the Robert she had known. He must. He could not have died completely. He had become comfortable, remote. They were no longer Harriet and Robert. They were just . . . people. She sat down on the edge of one of the twin beds. She always slept on Robert's right. She chose the right-hand bed.

"Dinner in five minutes," he said. His tone was jovial. He had accommodated himself, as usual.

"I'd almost rather starve," said Harriet. "Such a gruesome place. Why did we ever come here?"

"Business, business," said Robert. "You didn't have to come. We could have gone on to Torness, where my business really is. But you suggested it. Anyway, it'll be a nice drive tomorrow, along the coast road." It was one of the reasons she had given for stopping here, so they could enjoy the view in the morning.

"We should have gone on to Torness," said Harriet. "I believe there's a really good hotel there now, and a Fisherman's Wharf kind of restaurant."

"You should have thought of that before," said Robert. "It wasn't me that stuck a pencil into the map." He seemed to be enjoying himself, tying his tie and whistling between his teeth. A bell rang, sonorous and elderly. Doors opened and closed in the passage outside, and they heard murmured voices.

"Twenty years ago," said Harriet. "And I just remembered about the Fisherman's Wharf. It was in *The Queen*, last week."

"Yes. Well. We thought it would be fun," said Robert. He finished tying his tie. "Dinner?" he said, his head cocked.

"Alas, yes," said Harriet, and unwrapped the second cake of soap.

·

They came in late to the dining room. Gray heads turned in their direction, every shade of gray, from bluish iron to yellowish white, curled and puffed and marcelled. There was one other latecomer. She teetered about in the doorway, carrying an enormous embroidered knitting bag with wooden handles, and leaning heavily on a cane. The handles of the knitting bag caught somehow in the strap of Harriet's handbag. There was a moment of confusion.

"I'm *so* sorry, do excuse me." The bag opened, balls of yarn bounced softly away, trailing long tails that issued from the spiky nest of knitting needles in the bottom of the bag. Robert crawled about among the table legs, collecting the balls of wool, and returned them to the woman in the doorway. She smiled kindly at him, and tottered away across the dining room, the harsh light shining pinkly against her scalp, through her hair.

"The table in the corner, sir," said the waitress. She looked like an elderly cellist, short and square, with straight silver hair in a Dutch bob, and an improbable headdress of fluted pink linen. She and Harriet seemed equally out of place in a sea of tweed and Highland Fleck.

"We could go for a walk after dinner," said Harriet, and with an expression of fastidious distaste moved to one side the Dijon mustard and the covered sugar bowl. There was something quite awful about dining at a table where luncheons and teas were also served.

"Thick or clear?" said the waitress. Robert looked at her in surprise.

"Thick or clear what?"

"Don't be dense," said Harriet. "Soup, of course."

"Oh, yes. Hmm. I don't know. What do you recommend?"

"Recommend, sir?" The elderly cellist was surprised. "Well, there's just the thick and the clear, like. It depends on what you fancy."

"Thick," said Robert.

"Thin," said Harriet quickly. "I mean, clear." The waitress wrote it down and went away.

"I'd forgotten that," said Robert. "I didn't know anyone did it anymore."

"All that was old-fashioned when we first came here," said Harriet. "The whole place is a museum piece."

"Except that there weren't any choices at all," said Robert. "Sweet, really."

"I do believe you're enjoying yourself," Harriet remarked accusingly. "I believe this is the kind of life you'd really like to lead. The darling of the old ladies, the only man in the dining room."

"Why not?" said Robert. "It's all very safe and pleasant."

Harriet waited for a moment, while the waitress placed the soup before them. Then, "Do let's go for a walk after dinner," she said. Again, he ignored her.

·

They were married in winter, during the war, partly because Robert's leave came then, partly because Harriet and her mother had a penchant for winter finery, for furs and feathers, dark colors and rich fabrics. Harriet and her bridesmaids wore dark green velvet, and carried bouquets — prophetic, as it turned out — of prickly things, of holly, English and Chinese, of boxwood, and gray winter thistles. The florist thought the combination bizarre and probably unlucky. "Why not roses?" he asked mournfully. "I don't understand, honestly. Roses are so rich-looking. No, honestly. Show me something a white rose doesn't go with. Or lilies of the valley.

Now, they're pretty terrific, actually. No, honestly, they're so symbolic and everything. Or fuchsia, if you want color." He was getting a little frantic by that time. "I've got boxes coming up from Cornwall. Bleeding hearts, even. And some fern. Little sprays. Little *tiny* sprays . . ."

But if I had it to do over, thought Harriet, remembering what a pretty splash her wedding had made in the dull waters of the war, I'd do it exactly the same as I did then.

"How was the soup?" asked Robert. Harriet looked down at her plate in surprise. She hadn't noticed it, but she had finished it.

"I suppose it was all right," she said.

"Meat or fish?" said the waitress.

"What kind of meat? What kind of fish?" said Robert. He sounded distressingly arch, and glanced apologetically at Harriet.

"It's veal tonight, sir. Very nice. Or there's the haddock." Her tone disparaged the haddock.

"Veal, then," said Robert.

It came with a thick brown gravy, a large helping of inexpertly mashed potatoes, and another of haricot beans.

"Who do you suppose works in the kitchen?" said Harriet. "Serbs?"

"I shouldn't have bothered with the soup," said Robert. "It comes with the meat, anyway."

.

They quarreled for a variety of reasons. Harriet could not enjoy his making love to her, with the old ladies listening on either side of their room. She heard them hawking and coughing in the night, knew, or thought she knew, they were lying awake, listening for the creak of her bed, for the running of water in the washbasin, for her tiptoed visits across the hall to the bathroom. And yet, in the daytime, it was she who could not tear herself away from their company, who listened with a sort of fearful entrancement to their tales of mismatched couples, strawberry marks, imbecile children, and scandalous divorces. They did not often have a bride to talk to.

They gave her recipes for chocolate mousse and salmon in aspic, and poked their knitting needles in her ribs when they whispered about the marital relation. There was something about them that was both Victorian and Rabelaisian, and Harriet was fascinated. It was Robert who said he found the fug of the place impossible, who played irritatedly with the salt and pepper shakers at the breakfast table, and then flung out of the hotel, declaring the dining room to be stale and unhealthy, and went for long walks on the shingle. After a long moment, during which the swing door would sigh dejectedly back and forth, the old ladies would go on. "Four eggs at least, and a whole jug of cream." "He died, of course, and disinherited the lot of them." "Three children, or it might have been four, and every one a mongoloid idiot." And Harriet would break away, and run up to her room for her raincoat, and follow him, clambering down the cliff path which in the summer, they told her, was planted with geraniums and hydrangeas. The air was bleak, the sea gray and uninviting, Robert a small figure far ahead of her. The wind was incessant, but she ran through it, and caught up with him, her nose red and her eyes streaming, and linked her arm with his and complained that the cripples on the Esplanade

— pilots who had been shot down in the Battle of Britain —
were a bit too depressing, didn't he think? Somehow they
would come together, and Robert would disentangle his arm
from hers, and put it around her waist, and they would stagger
along the shingle together and like friends. They wondered
how the palm trees managed to survive, until they found out
the odd way in which the town was protected from the sea
wind by the headland, so that the air there was moist and
warm, and seemed saltless.

On one of their walks they came upon the abandoned
house, a long way up the beach.

.

"Not a honeymoon couple, are you, sir?" said the waitress.
She added hastily, "Excuse me. I know it's rather a personal
question, like, but the lady in the window wanted to know."

"I wonder what made her think we might be," said Harriet. She smiled around her, blessing anyone who might think
she and Robert a honeymoon couple.

"Daring youth. An air about us," said Robert. "Which
lady? Which window?" Again he sounded arch, almost like
an old lady himself, thought Harriet.

"That one, sir." The waitress inclined her head toward
a very old woman who sat nodding alone at a table among
the dark velvet curtains. It was the old lady who had dropped
the balls of knitting wool.

"Good Lord," said Robert. "Well, it's nice to know they
still take an interest. Tell her, no. No, we aren't."

Harriet felt suddenly sad, drowned in sadness, thinking
of the old house, and their walks there. The wind was always

blowing in that place, sand had sifted in, and there were large pebbles and dried seaweed on the floor, as though a high tide had carried them there. Boards rattled and doors banged. The roof creaked like the timbers of a ship.

·

"Red or white?" said the waitress.

"Wine?" said Harriet, surprised.

"It comes with the dinner." She poured two glasses of red.

"Veal is a moot point," said Robert. "And with this gravy . . ." Harriet drank, greedily.

"There's music in the lounge, after dinner," said the waitress, corking the bottle firmly.

"Delightful," said Robert. He and the waitress exchanged smiles.

"I thought we were going for a walk," said Harriet.

Robert shrugged. "If you prefer," he said. "But if I'm to be really fresh for the interview tomorrow . . . We still have to drive to Torness, you know."

"Music in the lounge, then," said Harriet. She felt bitter.

"Sweet or savory?" said the waitress. Robert looked at her questioningly.

"Sardines on toast, sir, or cabinet pudding." She seemed to have taken a fancy to Robert, a certain dislike to Harriet.

"We could have had that at The Copper Kettle," muttered Harriet, full of resentment.

"I don't think . . . No, neither, thank you," said Robert. "Just coffee."

"Black or white?" The waitress had the last word.

"Black, for both of us."

"A walk after dinner?" said Harriet. "Just a short one?" The waitress had not yet finished her laborious writing down, and looked at her hesitantly. "It isn't on the menu," said Harriet. "Just something I would like to do."

"The staff goes off at ten o'clock, madam," said the waitress, disapprovingly. "They lock the doors then. You'll have to get a key."

"You see," said Robert, with a queer kind of triumph. "You upset everybody." Harriet emptied the last of her wine, saying nothing. One of the pale blue paper streamers detached itself, floated down among the tables. There was a mild buzz of comment.

"Oh, dear," said the waitress. "Someone'll have to get after that."

.

They had made love there, really and truly, for the first time. The staircase came up in the middle of the top floor, like the stairway to a loft, and there were windows on all four sides. There was a glass-paneled door on the seaward side, warped tightly shut and cobwebbed over. No point in trying to open it. But outside was a tiny balcony. Someone had paced there. Someone had sat in a rocking chair. There were marks on the floor. It was like a loft, it was like a mill, it was like a sailing boat.

"I'm the captain of this ship," said Harriet. She shaded her eyes with her hand, and stared through the dusty window out to sea.

"No, I am," said Robert, and put his arms around her from behind.

"Look out, mate," she said, as he fumbled with her clothing. In those days, she thought, I had a sense of humor. "Buttons!"

After that, they made love there on the sandy floor a number of times. Harriet's remark became a sort of secret signal for them.

"I'm the captain of this ship," she would say, long after they had gone back to town, as she stood there in her white nightgown, next to the soft, wide bed, on the thick piled carpet. And, "No, I am," said Robert, coming on her like a galleon in full sail, a schooner, a fishing boat out of the mist, roused up by a secret dream, a private call. But it didn't last. It was something that had happened when they were brimful of energy and vitality, and looking forward with eagerness to the rest of their lives. Now, thought Harriet, we are forty. And it is all lost. It is not going to come again.

"Do you remember the old house?" she said, stirring her coffee.

"What old house?" said Robert. There the wind had played, the tussocks of grayish grass whipped and flattened in the sand, the dead leaves of the thistles rattled and threatened.

"The old house we used to explore. Don't you remember it, really?"

He hesitated. Then, "Oh, yes. Yes, I do. Well, of course, who wouldn't?" He gave her a look that was almost coy, and laid his hand on hers across the table. It was rather shocking, the gesture of a man who knows that something is expected of him, but no longer understands what it is.

"I thought we might go and see if it was still there," she said, a little forlornly. "But I expect it's gone, by now."

"Old places like that last forever," said Robert. "But it's a long way down the beach, as I remember." He stared off across the dining room for a moment. The old ladies were helping each other to their feet, retrieving canes and spectacle cases, setting themselves toward the doorway in a halting procession. Harriet watched him, a faint hope rising within her as he turned an odd, new, lost look on her. But then he said, "This hotel really *is* pretty comfortable, you know. Drink up your coffee, Harriet. Music in the lounge after dinner, remember?"

.

Music in the lounge was provided by a middle-aged woman playing the piano, and a bald, bespectacled man who sang a number of German lieder that all sounded alike.

"I like the way she kept her hat on," said Harriet, as they went upstairs afterward, moving with unnatural slowness, so as not to seem to bound before the rest of the company. "Sort of warning the poor man not to get too sentimental."

"Rousing fire in withered bosoms," said Robert. "Yes, that *was* tactful."

He seemed a little quiet and withdrawn as they prepared for bed, and he got into the wrong one, the one Harriet had mentally reserved for herself. Eventually they turned out the lights, and settled. Suddenly, startlingly, Robert got out of bed and climbed in beside Harriet.

"I'm the captain of this ship," he said.

Harriet hesitated for a moment. "No, I am," she said.

He hadn't got it right; he had it all wrong; but it didn't matter. They made love.

On the road to Torness in the morning, they passed the old house, but Harriet was busy lighting a cigarette for Robert, and neither of them noticed it.

The Lodge Pin

IN ALL THE SUBURBS, outside all the cities, the wives had gone shopping at the supermarkets, and the husbands were mowing the lawns. It was fall, one of the last times the mowing would need to be done. A Saturday morning, with a slight breeze blowing, cooling the faces and the armpits, ballooning out the sport shirts.

Hal Wakefield felt some slight answering stir within himself. It occurred to him that he hadn't made use of the summer, that soon the weather would change and he would be condemned to a life indoors, and he probably wouldn't make much use of the winter either. There was a lot to be said for fall. This was the kind of day that made him feel like going for a long walk, or would have, if there had been anywhere to walk to. But the subdivision spread wide in all directions, and Hal, carefully guiding the lawn mower against the chrysanthemums banked beneath the foundation plantings — four ligustrum, three arborvitae, two red cedars — wondered if anyone else found the name Glendale Woods as irritating as he did.

It had been wooded country once, but after the bulldozers

had got through, no one could tell whether it had been a glen or a dale, and maybe the two words meant the same thing anyway. The whole area looked exactly like Sunnyridge Hills, two or three miles down the road, though the houses were slightly different. And Sunnyridge Hills had been a completely flat piece of farmland, whatever the ads might say about rolling countryside. It hadn't rolled, it had simply spread out, part of the plain that lay between here and the river. In the old days, Hal supposed, you might have climbed a little rise, hidden now in the man-made topography of Glendale Woods but probably about where the shopping center is, and actually seen the river, gleaming in the distance. You might have packed a lunch and walked to its banks, seven miles away. Walked through the flat fields, beside the fences and hedges, past the farmhouses.

Just lately Hal had seen a print, an old wood engraving. It was part of an advertisement in the paper for the sale of men's casual clothing. It showed two men fishing from a river bank. They wore broad-rimmed hats, loose jackets, knee pants, and stockings. One of them lay on the ground and leaned on his elbow. The other, with a hare dangling from his pocket, leaned against a tree. They looked comfortable and as though they had all the time in the world. At the bottom of the picture, Hal could almost decipher a tiny signature. Thomas Something. Thomas was a friend, Hal thought. Obscurely saddened by the thought of the two men — they were quite real to him — folded now in his billfold, for he had torn the picture out of the paper and put it away, he pushed the lawn mower in a little too close and nicked the head off a chrysanthemum.

He picked it up, pungent-smelling, heavy headed, yellow petaled, and put it in his pocket. He would throw it away before Betsy got back from the supermarket, and she'd never miss it. It was another of the small things he kept from her.

More and more he kept things from her. Like what he felt about the children, about Jenny's marriage and John's being gone at college. About how he felt lonely and sad, and old, maneuvering the lawn mower in and out. About all the things he had wanted to do and knew now he never would, and knew his children wouldn't do them either and didn't even want to. Every time he read of a place that interested him, he added it to a secret list in his mind. Places I Would Like to See before I Die. He had never seen the Shiant Isles, the dashing waves beneath the rearing cliffs, never rested in an Alpine meadow, never stood on the banks of the Amazon. He sighed deeply, and his thoughts went to his daughter.

He had had such hopes for Jenny. They had given her music lessons because it was the thing to do. "Though, mind you," said Betsy, "it's just while she shows an interest. The minute she starts arguing about practicing, that's when we quit." But to the surprise of both of them, Jenny hadn't argued. She had practiced faithfully, and her teacher said she had great talent. Only a year or so before, when Hal heard the crashing chords beneath her fingers, he had seen her at Salzburg, reverently touching Mozart's clavichord despite the velvet rope and all the notices. He heard her in Bayreuth, arguing during an intermission of the opera *Parsifal*, speaking German with a group of students. He saw her wearing woolen stockings and a short skirt, tramping over the mountains, and this seemed to him the best vision of all.

All these things might have happened, but Jenny had married. Her husband, Bob, was doing all right, of course. There was nothing to worry about. They had met in Pittsburgh, where Jenny was studying, and Bob had been doing all right even then, working in his father's automobile agency, and now he had set up for himself and come along just fine. They were living in an apartment on the other side of town and were saving up for a down payment on one of the houses in Sunnyridge Hills. Betsy was just tickled about it, and Hal knew he should be pleased. Instead, and dumbly, he resented it. Their lives seemed to be following such a pattern. There was none of the embroidery he had hoped for. And even though he and Betsy had given Jenny a baby grand of her own for a wedding present, she hardly ever played anymore, except college songs when a group of young people came over.

He didn't understand Jenny, and he didn't understand himself. He felt they had been a great deal too anxious to see her married, as though there was nothing better in life for a girl than to marry the first possible young man who came along. Nothing better for the young man, if it came to that, than to find a little wife and have a little baby and put them both in a little box in Sunnyridge Hills, Glendale Woods, Shadey Acres, Forest Lawn Estates.

Maybe it would have been better if Jenny and Bob had just had an affair for a while and got it out of their systems. Hal blushed in the light wind and ran his handkerchief around the back of his neck, because he had just had a thought that if it weren't immoral he didn't know what it was; he knew how Betsy would feel if he should say it out loud. But he couldn't help thinking it, he told himself defiantly, and put away his handkerchief. And wasn't a love affair, happy or unhappy, less narrowing for a person than marriage in a vacuum? Cut-and-dried marriage? Assembly-line marriage? At least you *knew* when it was over, and you had an experience you could think about and learn from. And there were a lot of worries you didn't have, like its *never* being over, or if it were, the sharing out of furniture, hi-fi records, and children, too, maybe. And Jenny could have gone back to college and been the success he had always hoped she would be, instead of just sitting around singing college songs with a lot of other young marrieds.

These were thoughts he had to keep from Betsy, had to keep in his own head, pushing the lawn mower back and forth under the maple trees at the back of the house, because no one would be on his side in an argument like that. They would all be on the other side, the side he'd read about in a book by an explorer. The most important thing in life, wrote the explorer, was the creation of a happy family life. He had described for hundreds of pages the extraordinary pleasures of discovering new parts of the world, of having been the first man to set eyes on this valley or that mountain. And then he had said that none of it was important. Compared with a happy family life, nothing weighed in the scales, not a career, not adventure nor discovery, certainly not a man himself. Hal crossed the frozen wastes of Antarctica off his list at that. He didn't want to go where that man had been.

He saw that Joe Durham, who lived across the street, was mowing his lawn too and had stopped to wave to him. He waved back and grinned uncomfortably, wondering if Joe had seen him put the chrysanthemum in his pocket. It seemed

like a funny thing to do. After all, he could have taken it inside and put it in a glass of water.

He went on mowing at the same moment Joe did, thinking
how strange it was that though he knew everybody who lived
around him and they all knew him, he was lonely all the
same. It seemed to Hal sometimes that something had gone
wrong with his life. He couldn't think what it could be. It
wasn't anything you could put your finger on, and whatever
it was, no one else seemed to feel it, though his life was just
the same as theirs. He had, quite often, the sensation of being
a stranger in a foreign country, of their ways not being his
ways, yet of not being able to identify the country he was in.
Sometimes he actually felt the *excitement* and the difference
of being in a foreign country, as though the smells, the heat,
the dust of Glendale Woods were all strange to him. When
he got caught up in the great traffic jam going into the city
each morning, he was sometimes visited by the same sense
of strangeness and aloneness. Where was everyone going?
Where had they come from? The only compensation was
that as he wove in and out of the traffic, shifting from the
right to the left lane at exactly the right moment, he felt he
was pretty well acclimatized, considering that he was a
stranger. He could drive as well as they could.

What was the difference? In his childhood he had walked
to school, just as they had. His life had the same beginnings
as theirs; none of this yellow bus nonsense. Everyone had
done it. They sometimes vied with each other, talking about
how far they had walked and how deep the snow had been,
agreeing that nowadays children were soft, didn't know how
well off they were.

"I was about to get frostbitten once," he had said just the other night. They were sitting out on the patio, one of the last times they would do it now that summer was gone, the husbands and wives from this small corner of the subdivision drinking beer. Every now and then someone got up and left to check on sleeping children.

"I was walking along the lane from school, and the snow was this deep." He held his hand out, palm down, to indicate just how deep. "Well, maybe not that high, but over my head anyway. I couldn't have been more than six years old. I know I'd just started school. I was so cold, and I was walking slower and slower, just hoping, you know, that someone would come and get me, just about ready to lie down in the snow and go to sleep. And then the door to this house opened and a woman came out and made me go inside with her. She had a great big fire going, and there was a cat with some kittens in a basket. She wouldn't let me go near the fireplace, but she gave me some cookies. And then you know what she did? She took off my shoes and socks and stuck my feet in a bucket of ice water. I thought she was a witch." He felt foolish when he'd finished the story because he felt there was some significance in it, that he'd come so close to getting frostbitten feet and been so shocked by the cure, but the others didn't seem to get it. They just laughed and said they'd never heard of ice water as a cure for frostbite.

.

The lawn mower hit a rock, and Hal swore. He'd given the next-door youngster fifty cents to go over the lawn and throw out every rock he found and anything else that shouldn't be there. The house was on a corner, and sometimes there were beer cans thrown on the front lawn. Teen-agers driving by at night. Sometimes they threw beer cans, paper cups — all kinds of trash — right on the front lawn. They took the corner so fast, often he woke up in the night and heard them screech by. He lived in fear that someday one of them would drive right across his yard and smash into the corner of the house. Brick veneer. It wouldn't take a crash like that. He could see it clearly, his house with a great hole in it, and the upper floor sagging into the lower; beds and chests of drawers sliding out into the foundation plantings, broken bricks strewn about. He didn't know what he would do if a thing like that happened.

Throwing the rock out into the street, he wondered if he'd been the same when he was young. He was almost sure he hadn't. It seemed to him that about that time, just about the time he went to college, he'd been quick, intelligent, full of power, seeking and finding. He thought he'd never been so alert since. And the long winters. He had made use of the winters in those days, gone skiing and skating. Gone on sledding parties and studied in a cold room. The girls, the girls were different then, too. Rosier, rounder. Their cute little fur hats, their mittened hands.

·

He came to the place on the lawn where the telescope had stood. Packed away in the basement now, it belonged to his son, John. A telescope was the thing to give your boy, right after Sputnik. Everyone had one, even little kids, and Hal made sure he got a good one. A book on astronomy came with it, with charts that told you when you could see the different constellations. He and John had set the tripod up on the lawn in front of the living room window.

"I had a telescope once," Hal told his son, "an old mariner's telescope. I used to sit on the window seat in my room and stare at the sky for hours."

"You couldn't have seen much," said John, efficient, turning screws this way and that. "Not with an old instrument like that. What were you looking for?"

"I don't know," said Hal. "God, maybe." He was suddenly annoyed with the new telescope, a sinister and clinical-looking object, compared with the worn, familiar, brassbound instrument of his childhood.

For a few nights John was sufficiently interested to spend an hour or so identifying the planets and looking at the craters on the moon.

"Say, Dad, this is a pretty good telescope!" he said, as though Hal had bought a good one by accident. Then he took to lowering the telescope to bring the house of a friend up the street leaping into his eye. He said he could see Mike, his best friend, studying in a pair of green-striped pajamas. He said Mike had a new desk lamp with a gooseneck, and could he have one too. John meant no harm, but it was the sort of thing you got arrested for, Hal thought uneasily, and he was glad when John lost interest in the telescope. Then he himself took it up, and he found Saturn. Saturn, with its silver rings, floating high in blackness, in lonely majesty. Cold with a cold unimagined, taking twenty-nine years to circle the sun. He watched it for a long time, spellbound.

"It looks like — like a lodge pin, set in black velvet," he told John, trying to impart some of his enthusiasm. And it did. A lodge pin, the emblem of some godly fraternity, there in the sky. But John was bored, looked through the telescope in a perfunctory fashion, and nodded his head briefly. Hal wasn't sure that John had even seen Saturn. Surely no one who had could tear himself away so soon? Cold, cold, ringed with silver and very far away. And yet *Saturnia Regna.* The Golden Age, filled with all delights. Saturn had been thrown out of heaven by his son Jupiter, and gone to Italy and reigned there. Hal heaved a great sigh when he thought of this.

Joe Durham came over one night to ask him if they could see *Echo,* but it moved too fast, and they watched it for a while without bothering with the telescope, which stood like a black finger on three legs, pointing bleakly at the sky.

"Isn't that something?" said Joe. "I guess the old USA has something after all."

"Yeah," said Hal. He wondered why he couldn't feel as enthusiastic about the satellite as other people did. It didn't seem to have too much to do with him, somehow, though in another way it had too much to do with him and was another worry added to all the rest. One day the sky would be so full of the damned things you wouldn't be able to see the stars. They would have to have traffic rules. This way around. Do not pass. Seven spacemen killed on this curve in 1970.

When Joe went back across the street, Hal took another look at Saturn and found its lonely state soothing and wonderful.

·

He had finished doing the lawn now and put the lawn mower away, just as Betsy drove up the driveway. He opened the door for her, and together they carried the grocery bags into the kitchen, and he washed his hands at the sink while she put things away. He was very conscious of the chrysanthemum in his pocket, feeling like a secret drinker come upon with a half-full glass still to dispose of, and he wished Betsy would go out, turn her back for a minute so that he could get rid of it. When she went out to the car to get something she had forgotten, he dropped it in the trash and covered it with a crumpled paper bag, wondering why he couldn't tell her quite simply and easily that he had cut the head off one of the flowers or, better yet, hand it to her and say he had picked it especially for her. A memory stirred in him of having done the same thing in his childhood. Pulled the head off a flower and given it with a smile to his exasperated mother. The truth was, he thought, as Betsy came back into the kitchen, that he didn't want to hear what she had to say. He was fond of her, but he didn't much like to hear her talk about anything.

She was talking now about John, saying she would bake up a batch of cookies and send them to him; she was sure he must be starved, she knew how haphazard he was about eating. A hamburger here, a milk shake there; that was no way to keep healthy.

"Cookies?" said Hal. "According to you, what he needs is a steak dinner. Preferably three times a day."

"Well, I know," said Betsy. She smiled the smile that had wrung him in his youth, irritated him in the present. Acknowledging her fault. "But they'll fill him up. That's better than nothing." She made coffee and sank down opposite Hal at the kitchen table.

"You finished the lawn."

"Yeah," said Hal.

"I was beginning to get worried," said Betsy. "You know how the next-door people are about wind-blown seeds."

"The grass wasn't that high."

"You got it just in time," she said. Over her coffee cup her eyes roved about the kitchen. "It's quiet. Quiet without the children. Nobody here but us, I mean." Hal nodded without speaking, and she smiled and touched his hand.

"It's like old times," she said. "As we were."

"As we were," said Hal.

"We've got a lot to be proud of," said Betsy. "Both of them gone and settled. You hear so much about wild kids nowadays. I say we have a lot to be proud of." There was a slight reprimand in her voice.

"I am," said Hal. Was he?

"You don't sound very proud," said Betsy. She cleared away the coffee cups with small annoyed movements. "I don't know what you want out of life, Hal. Sometimes I just don't understand you." He didn't particularly want to be understood, but he felt panic all the same.

"The revolt of the middle-aged man," he offered, and when she failed to smile, "it's the title of a book." And hastily, in case she should think he had been seduced by unsuitable literature, "I didn't read it."

"You used to have so much pep," said Betsy. "New ideas all the time." She shook her head and suddenly smiled, wringing out a dishcloth over the sink. "Wore me out, almost. I guess I shouldn't complain, just so long as you don't start chasing around after any young women." The smile was beamed directly at him, inviting him to share the joke, and Hal was quite startled. It occurred to him that he hadn't seen

any young women around, not for years now, except his own
daughter of course, and where had they all gone to?

"Now, Betsy," he said. She wiped the sink top, while his
mind dredged up one young woman after another and dis-
charged them, while he thought there was a whole facet of
life he had never really thought to explore.

"You could fix the washing machine," said Betsy. "It jiggles
all over the floor. You could level it."

"Sure," said Hal.

"Jenny and Bob are coming over tomorrow for Sunday dinner," she said. "I think Jenny's got some news for us."

"A baby?"

Betsy nodded, smiling.

"Well, how do you like that?"

"There's a whole trunkful of old things of Jenny's down in
the basement. Toys, baby clothes, and things. I wish you'd
get it out for me, Hal. I told Jenny she should look through
it and take some of those things for the baby."

●

Hal went down to the basement and got a screwdriver off the
bench. He opened up the door to the crawl space under the
house, which they used for storage since there was no attic,
and hauled out the old trunk. It slipped from his grasp as he
was setting it down on the floor, and the snap lock flew up.
Idly, Hal lifted the lid and looked down at the contents.
Glimpses of lace, white cotton, pink and blue woolly things.
A teddy bear and two or three dolls. A Monopoly set, a shell
collection, and a microscope. He stood looking down at it.
It had hardly been used. He'd given it to Jenny when she was

in eighth grade, or thereabouts, so she could do a project for the school science fair. Something to do with animal hair, he thought. He'd taken Jenny to the zoo and daringly plucked at a monkey's fur for her. A tuft had come away in his hand as though he'd pulled it from an old fur coat, and she had added it to her collection of specimens. When they looked at the monkey's fur under the microscope, they found it was full of tiny insects and even tinier eggs.

"Parasites," said Hal. Betsy made a noise of disgust.

"Lice," she said. "Throw the dirty stuff away. Burn it."

"And I suppose those parasites have parasites on *them*," said Hal. "And on and on. Too small to be seen even by the most powerful microscope. And even in the smallest one there are millions of atoms, spinning around, that make up its shape."

He was fascinated by the idea, and it had given rise to another one. It had rather frightened him, and he didn't say anything about it until one evening when he heard Jenny and John arguing about religion.

"So every word in the Bible is true," scoffed John. "And Abraham lived to be eight hundred years old, and the Red Sea parted down the middle just to let the Jews out of Egypt. Nobody believes that stuff anymore."

"That's not a nice way to talk, John," said Betsy.

"Some people do," said Jenny. "Thousands of them. They can't all be wrong."

"Thousands of people can be just as wrong as one person," said John loftily. "Science has disproved the Bible. Certain things just can't happen. Don't you believe in the laws of nature?"

"God exists," said Hal suddenly.

"Of course," said Betsy, relieved. "Foolish nonsense."

"But I wonder if He knows *we* exist," said Hal, and the children looked at him. "I wonder if He's discovered us yet. Have you ever thought about how small we are? I mean, when you look up at the sky, have you ever thought that? When you look at Saturn, say?"

"The one you said looked like a lodge pin," said John. If he was being sarcastic, Hal didn't notice.

"That's exactly it. And then, when you look into the microscope, have you ever thought how *big* we are? Can you imagine that the entire universe might be no bigger than a lodge pin? Smaller, even. A little diamond chip that God wears." They looked puzzled and a little bored. Betsy, knitting, wasn't even listening.

"Oh, Dad," said John. Hal shrugged.

"Just an idea," he said. He could have put it much better, he thought. There wasn't necessarily any end to it either. There might be a God a million times greater than God.

.

"Did you get the trunk out?" said Betsy. She came down the basement steps. "Oh, look at that!" she exclaimed, and knelt lovingly beside the shrine of Jenny's childhood. She took out one of the knitted jackets and held it to her face. "Just as soft. You'd think it was bought yesterday. And all those little gowns. Jenny won't have to get many new things."

"Toys too," said Hal. "He can play with those. Some of them, anyway," disparaging the dolls.

"It might be a girl."

"Yeah. Fifty-fifty. Could be either one. You want me to leave the trunk right here?"

"Why don't you? And Jenny can take out whatever she wants."

"I don't guess she'll want this," said Hal, and picked up the microscope. "You know, I think I'll take this upstairs. And John's old telescope, too."

"You don't want that stuff," said Betsy. "Where will you put it? It'll just sit around, gathering dust."

"It's going to do that in the crawl space," said Hal. "Maybe we should sell those things. Or give them away."

"Oh, well," said Betsy vaguely. She started up the stairs. "Leave them where they are. They might come in useful sometime."

And that was an example of real clear thinking, Hal thought, as he screwed the door back in place and closed the lid of the trunk. What kind of usefulness did she have in mind, and who would use the telescope and the microscope if he didn't and she didn't and John and Jenny didn't? But he didn't fret himself about it. It was the kind of thing that happened every day.

And when we've blown ourselves up, he thought, continuing the idea he had had before, God won't even notice. There'll just be the smallest possible flaw in the diamond.

·

Late that night he was roused from sleep by a long-remembered sound. He raised himself on an elbow, and his spirits rose and followed. It was the night wind, harbinger of winter, sweeping down over the mountains of his childhood, rushing over the tops of enormous trees. For a moment he thought he was, after all, an inhabitant of a mysterious and beautiful world. But the sound altered, changed, and died away. Long before it had ceased altogether, Hal knew he was listening to a train rumbling over a distant bridge. He sank back into sleep, an unimportant man in a dark suburban bedroom, conveniently close to the shopping center, the highway, and the railroad station.

Constance

CONNIE. CONSTANCE. It all depended on how he was feeling, and she had been Connie for years now. Sometimes, even, just — Con. Con Siebold, his wife. Walter thought about her all the way on the plane. Or rather, all the way on the plane he tried not to think about her. But she clung to his mind like a burr to a piece of cloth, attached by a hook so delicate and yet so strong that not even the most massive blow could dislodge it. He knew this perfectly well, and yet he had never been able to train himself to do other than deliver to that portion of his mind where she clung what were, in effect, massive blows, and quite ineffectual.

He thought about her with forced scorn, about how heavy she had grown, how ugly, her large round bosom straining against flowered cotton as she leaned over in the seat of the car, about how foolish she was, how extravagant, though once she had had a saving streak that was maddening to him. He thought, quite innocently, that if she had had any sense she would have known she could have come on this trip with him, whatever he said, and that whatever he said was because he didn't want her along.

Sometimes it passed through his mind that there were other, more delicate lines of thought, through which he might detach her from himself, but he lacked the almost surgeonlike precision and courage he would need in such a venture, and could only quail at the image of himself dying, a tree deprived of the protection of the vine.

He remembered he had said he would go to King Street.

Connie had put her hand on his arm as he was getting out of the car at the airport. She leaned over in the driver's seat, her face close to his, powdery and large and earnest, though Walter did not look at her face, but vaguely at the flowered mass of her.

"Go and take a look at King Street, while you're there," she said. "Remember, the old place?" He had moved his head with annoyance, and frowned his refusal. Connie had straightened up and looked away from him and said how much she would like to see it again. Someone she knew drove by, a neighbor, and despite the immediate problem she waved, with the sudden, surprised, enchanted smile that irritated him because it accorded so ill with the rest of her. He was doubly irritated to recognize, with her words and her smile, an immediate mental image of the old place on King Street, the broken-down sofa, the corner of an enamel kitchen table, a square of batik on the wall, and the light from the window shining on Connie's head as she bent over a grocery list.

"All right," he said, shrugging. "If I have time."

He didn't have much time in New York, and in order to do as Connie wanted, he had to leave the last meeting early, though in fact it broke up with his departure. He murmured something about getting a present for his wife, and because the speech he'd made had been successful, some of the men came out with him, talking about the points he had raised, riding down in the elevator with him, and standing around him in a little cluster while he got a cab.

He waved his farewells, calling out that he would see them again that night, at the dinner. He hadn't been to New York for the firm before, but he'd been to other cities, and it was always the same. There was always a dinner, and then a few of them got together and went to a nightclub, and there were girls. Walter looked back at the men, standing in a small aggressive knot on the sidewalk, and told himself it had been all right to say that about getting a present for his wife, it wouldn't make any difference, they would still see there was a girl for him. These things didn't always turn out right. He hoped for a bit better than the one he'd had last time — in Dallas was it, or Detroit? She'd been too young for him, too sassy, and she'd ended up laughing at him. She said something about his being a mother's boy, needing his mother, not a girl. She wouldn't get very far with an attitude like that, he knew, but he'd been furiously angry with her. All because he'd told her about his miserable youth, cried on her shoulder a little, complained about Con a little. It was an uncomfortable memory, but a small one, so he dismissed it, and leaning back in the cab thought instead about Connie's asking him to go to King Street.

He thought it was a little like the story in which the favorite daughter asks her father to bring her back one white rose from his travels. No length of embroidered silk for her, no golden slippers, no casket of jewels. Just a single white rose. It was supposed to show how unselfish and sweet the favorite daughter was, but Walter wondered if the father hadn't found it a difficult and frustrating request. Perhaps it was the wrong time of year for roses, probably they didn't even grow in the region he was going to, or it could have been that white roses just weren't being grown that year, pink and red being the more fashionable colors.

Why hadn't Con asked for rolls of fine silk, or their equivalent? God knew, the city had everything. There was in fact an alligator handbag in his overnight bag in the hotel room, that had set him back seventy-five dollars, and a flask of perfume that cost almost as much. But these, he admitted to himself, were things the businessman in a hurry could find in his lunch hour, in almost any store. Connie wanted her white rose, the visit to King Street, and Walter thought how typical of her it was.

The thought of giving flowers to a woman brought to his mind an occasion long ago, years before Connie. He had gone calling on a girl, with a bunch of flowers in his hand. He noticed when he got to her house that they had all wilted, and he remembered dunking the whole thing into a rain bucket outside the back porch, and then running up the wooden steps and hammering on the kitchen door. The flowers hadn't been worth giving anyone; they had made him look a fool, though he had gathered them carefully enough, in his mother's yard. The girl had seen them anyway, as they started out on their usual walk, and even though he'd dodged and sidled and tried to screen the rain bucket from her, she'd known at once the flowers had been intended for her, and laughed and teased him. He had cursed the tissue paper and the ribbon his mother had wrapped around the stems, which made them into a present, and not just some old flowers that had somehow fallen into the water. It was like his mother to do that. They got along badly; she never let him do a thing he ever really wanted, and, in all kinds of small ways that looked like generous attentions, she contrived to spoil his life for him. She had been dead for twenty years, and he rarely thought of her, but when he did he didn't forgive her either, for the tissue paper and the ribbon. He was really crazy about that girl, but his mother had to put her oar in. She had worked hard to be able to send him to college, but he remembered more clearly how she'd made him comb his hair in the way she considered most gentlemanly, and wear clothes he didn't like.

The neighborhood was becoming more familiar to him, and in the cab Walter leaned forward and looked out at the stores and the people lining the sidewalks, and craned his neck to read the street signs. There, he saw with sudden excitement, was the place where they used to buy bread, he and Constance. The little Viennese bakery, with its warm scent of yeast and bread rising, and special cakes on Sundays and holidays. Whoever owned it now had enlarged the place, extended it into the property next door. There were plate glass windows, rows of cakes and rolls, tiered stands loaded with petit fours, apple turnovers laid out like little buttery corpses on doilies of paper lace. Walter remembered it as the place where that old man — he was always That Old Man, The Old Viennese — had placed, so carefully, slices of fresh strudel into white paper bags for him to take home to Constance, for Constance to take home to him. When they had no money they had stood outside, like baby birds waiting for a handout. And Constance had got crusty long loaves there, and always came home with stories about him. The Old Viennese. Old Franz Schubert. The place hadn't changed hands after all. On the sign above the store, Walter read SCHUBERT'S BAKERY.

The drugstore was not much changed. There they had bought the reams of paper, the pencils and erasers and typewriter ribbons that would one day turn him into a famous writer, or so Constance believed. What a crazy idea. Walter shook his head and sat back in the cab, regretting the time he had wasted. Those crazy ideas. Con sure had done a snow job on him in those days, persuading him of talents he didn't have, of possibilities that didn't exist.

The cab turned a corner, and the driver told him, "King Street, mister. Any particular number?" Walter was so surprised by the change in King Street that he didn't answer, but let the driver take him past the house he was looking for, and slow down in the middle of the block.

"What number did you want?" said the driver.

"You can let me out right here," said Walter. "It's a short street. I'll find it." He counted out change and got out of the cab, and watched the driver move off in an irritated arc, describing a U-turn where there was a sign clearly proclaiming NO U-TURNS.

The place had changed. For a place that was as run-down as King Street had been, twenty, twenty-three years ago, it certainly had changed. And yet there was something familiar about the changes, as though he had known they would be there, and had simply forgotten about them. New paint. Every one of the houses was spruce with new paint. Bow windows and balconies had been added, geraniums in pots on the windowsills. Everything so clean, no litter at all, even the sidewalk looked swept.

Walter walked slowly back in the direction from which the taxi had brought him, looking at the numbers over the doors. A young girl in stretch slacks, a black sweater and panther-spotted slippers came out of one of the houses and went hurrying off down the street. She was slim and young, and attractively dressed, but Walter, groping for a cigarette, saw in her swinging hair Constance as she had been long ago, going out of the house to shop in the little stores around the corner.

He came to the house he was looking for. He looked twice at the number, and then at the numbers on either side, just to be sure. A pink door, with the kind of paint one knew had not been applied yesterday or the day before, but which would nevertheless and unobtrusively be kept looking exactly as it was. A bronze knocker in the shape of a mermaid. A small tree in a green tub on either side of the entrance. A wrought iron handrail. Walter stood for a moment, light-ing his cigarette. He couldn't remember what had been there before, before the bronze mermaid. A cheap, scabbed, flaky piece of metal, that gave off a cheap, flaky sound against the dull brown door. They had had a bell too, the button hang-ing out of its socket, with the wires exposed. It worked, if you were patient, but no one ever used it. As well as the mermaid knocker, he supposed, there would be some more private way of being admitted to the house, a neat little but-ton that sounded a quiet buzzer upstairs, but from where he stood he couldn't see it.

The door opened, and a woman came out. Walter dropped

his lighter, and bent down to pick it up. She was gray-haired, about as old as Con, or older, but she hadn't let herself go, she was well dressed in a gray-flecked tweed suit, and stood up straight. She gave him a sharp look as she closed the door behind her, as though she had some suspicion of him, and walked away in the same direction as the girl in slacks. Walter wondered how long she had lived there, and if it would occur to her that she hadn't shut the door properly behind her, she'd been so busy looking at the strange man outside her house.

He was inside almost as soon as she was out of sight, standing in the narrow hall that was so familiar and yet so unfamiliar. Striped wallpaper, a mirror, a little white-painted table beneath it, an ashtray, a pair of gloves.

I must be crazy, he thought. What made me do a thing like that? And she'll come back for her gloves. He glanced at the stairs, and decided he might as well look at the whole place while he was there. He stubbed out his cigarette carefully in the ashtray, and ran up on light feet. The stair carpet was unfamiliar, but the stairs themselves so well remembered that he almost called out, "Constance!" on the third one from the top, and half expected her to appear from the doorway on the left, wearing that damned purple jacket, her gray skirt that hung down on one side, and an apron. There wasn't anyone there, and as he crushed the almost instinctive feeling of her presence that made him want to call her again, to explain why he was late, why he hadn't come home earlier, he also experienced a streak of quite rational fear, as he wondered what the hell he would have said if there *had* been anyone there.

I must be crazy, he told himself again, but he stood looking around the room at the top of the stairs. "I used to live here," he said aloud, to the pictures on the walls, to the bowl of flowers, to the desk under the window. It was all changed, nothing was the same. It was all pretty, light, and orderly. Someone else's life was here, and the life he and Constance had was all swept away.

And yet here too the changes were familiar, as they were in the street outside, even to details like the five or six old photographs in oval frames, strung one above the other on a black ribbon on the wall. He remembered how it had been, so bare, the only decoration that square of batik pinned over a stain on the plaster above the sofa, and a poster advertising a bullfight, something someone had brought back from Mexico, and apart from that nothing but the typewriter, and the chipped coffee pot, and the little radio with the wires crawling all over the place, standing on the white enamel table they'd bought at an auction for a dollar fifty. Walter experienced a feeling so sad and strange that, if it had still been there, he would have thrown himself down on the old broken-down sofa, covered in monk's cloth at forty cents a yard, special.

He felt like someone who has been shut away from the world for a long time, and forgotten that it existed. Like a prisoner on the day of his release, when he stands bewildered on the street, and sees it full of strangers, brighter, smarter, happier than he had remembered people to be; people he had started out in step with, who had gone on to lives full of incident and event, while he had stood still in one place, and nothing at all had happened to him. The feeling angered him, because it wasn't true. He had got out of the trap that was King Street, he had gone into business, he had made a success of his life, he had all the things that other people had, the things he had wanted so badly when he was young, and thought he would never achieve, the houses and cars and swimming pools, the important little jobs in big firms. Almost, he had thrown them all away when he married Constance. There had been a little money, she had been brought up in a different way. She thought in terms of boarding a freighter to go to Europe, of helping the Greeks when the war was over, of sitting up all night to finish a poem, or a bottle of cheap Mexican brandy. Externals didn't matter to her. Personal sloppiness was a symbol of inner striving. Practicing no art herself, she wanted more than anything to be attached to a man who did. While he was in the army, her parents died, and when he came out he had, with rare determination, accepted the money left her — not much, but enough to start him in a business. But he hadn't forgotten his debt to Constance. She had — and a quiet wave of exultation broke over him — a little income of her own, thanks to his generosity and success. Sloppy, unattractive, and, he thought, beaten, she had that. Though he couldn't imagine what she did with it, she seemed never to have anything, had been extravagant, invested unwisely, gave away foolish and ostentatious presents. He didn't care, he really didn't care, and he never inquired.

He gave a final glance around the room, so neat and trim and comfortable, noting the embroidery on the seats of the chairs, the airy curtains, a flowered cup and saucer, a figurine and a jade animal behind glass in a little cabinet, and started down the stairs. In the hall he emptied the ashtray in his pocket, and wiped it clean with his handkerchief. He walked out as easily as he had walked in. He was out on the sidewalk again, looking at the ornamental trees. Several people went by, but no one paid any attention to him, and the gray-haired woman hadn't come back for her gloves.

Suddenly he knew why everything was so familiar to him. All the changes were things Constance had wanted to do. "When you make some money, we'll paint the front door pink," she said, "and put two little trees — orange trees — in tubs, outside. Walter, do orange trees bear in captivity?" Looking through an envelope full of old photographs — stuff he had got from his mother, that she had got from *her* mother — she said, "I'd like to have them in little oval frames, and hang them here, on a black ribbon with a bow at the top."

He had wondered why she gave any thought to a future in that place, why she felt King Street was home. To him, it was poverty-stricken and hateful, and when Constance admired the little house, spoke of how she would bring out its good proportions, flatter its less interesting features, he thought she was talking nonsense. He still thought so. He glanced up once more at the windows. Just the same. They had been happy there, for a moment. In the beginning. And slowly he walked to the corner, where he could get a cab.

He didn't know when it was that he'd begun, systematically, to destroy Constance, but he remembered very well the argument about the purple jacket. It was, he thought, the first argument they had ever had, and even then Constance hadn't argued with him, not really. He had had it all to do by himself. As he watched her put it on for the thousandth time, anger had suddenly erupted in him.

"Don't you have any other clothes? Does that thing ever

go to the cleaners, even?" And she said she hadn't, and it didn't.

"It's my favorite thing. Don't you like it?" And since before that Walter had always liked everything about her, her face had an uncertain look. But he had taken a good look at their finances that day, and he knew they weren't going to make it. But it wasn't fair, he told the lost-and-long-ago Constance. It wasn't fair. You tried to build me up into something I wasn't, make something out of nothing. Remembering her standing there, in front of that square of batik that meant something, some artistic aspiration and declaration he'd never been clear about, wearing her lopsided flannel skirt, he had to grin. We were the beatniks of our day, he told himself. We never had more than one outfit at a time.

"I can't stand it," he said about the jacket, and lay down spitefully, with his shoes up on the monk's cloth–covered sofa, while she fiddled with that awful bag she carried, took everywhere with her, even from one room to another, a black-dyed calfskin clutch affair she'd made in an art class in the tenth grade.

"Purple for sentimentality, dirty for sluttishness," he said about the jacket.

With that terrible innocence of hers, she'd promised to have it cleaned. She hadn't wanted to spend the money, she said earnestly, since she was saving to buy things for the house, but if that was what he wanted, if he really thought . . .

He hadn't started having affairs with other women for some years. Affairs, he knew then and later proved, cost money. But he had already stopped loving Constance. The phrase stopped him. Loving Constance. At one time it had been his whole life and hope. Loving Constance. Of course he had grown out of it. He had forced himself to grow out of it. And yet, in other women what had attracted him? What was he trying to prove? He would catch a glimpse of something he seemed to recognize, but it always vanished before he could identify it. Sometimes it was like looking at a reflection of himself, when he felt particularly assured and self-confident, but the light changed and the glass shattered before he could be sure, and the affairs remained just that — affairs, little businesses of the body, with him picking up the scraps and shards and fragments of himself, after the rare occasions when they had promised to be more.

Thinking of all this, he felt again the growth of obscure rage. Constance had been unfaithful to *him*. Not physically, not with any man, but in not needing to be reflected in him, as he needed to be in her. Like the traveler who had three daughters, there was a woman attached to him who asked nothing of him, and it made him angry and impatient. Still, he had got out of there, he had looked around, got an offer, made his way, and his stupid unfulfilled youth was behind him. He, Walter Siebold, was something of a personage, after all.

At the end of the street, right on the corner, was a real estate agent's office. Donovan and Fine. On an impulse, Walter turned, and pushed open the door.

A prim-mouthed, elderly man sat behind a desk.

"That house, number sixteen-o-three. Do you carry that? Is it for sale?" said Walter. He thought he might persuade the gray-haired woman who had gone out without her gloves, and without properly latching the door, to sell it. It was the kind of place where a person might settle. A novel might be written there. A book of poems.

"We do carry it on our books, yes, sir," said the man, "but it isn't for sale." He got down a blue-bound book, and consulted it.

"I think I saw the lady who owns it," said Walter, carefully. "Don't you think she might be persuaded to sell?"

"Mrs. Siebold?" said the agent. "I don't think you can have seen her, sir. She lives in California. Just let me . . ." He leafed through the book on the desk. "Yes. Mrs. Walter Siebold owns that house. She's renting it to a single lady. Maybe that's the woman you saw."

"How long has she owned it?" said Walter. The primmouthed man looked at him.

"For how many years? About twelve, I fancy. Yes. Twelve years. Of course I could contact her. But I don't mind telling you . . . What was your name, sir?"

"Walter," said Walter.

"I don't mind telling you, Mr. Walter, the last offer we had was for fifty thousand dollars. Mrs. Siebold turned it down. She intends to hang on to that property. Yes, sir." Walter didn't know which piece of information made him angrier, the knowledge that Connie owned the house on King Street, or the discovery that she had turned down an offer of fifty thousand dollars for it.

"I could find you something else," said the agent. "There's a house just across the street — of course, only one bath."

"Tell Mrs. Walter Siebold," said Walter, "tell her, when you're next in touch with her, that house is grossly overpriced.

I wouldn't touch it with a ten-foot pole." The agent turned up his hands.

"Well," he said deprecatingly. "Sentimental older women. I understand Mrs. Siebold lived there herself when she was young. It may hold happy memories for her."

"I expect it does," said Walter, "but you can't cash in on happy memories." He stood there for a moment, wondering.

"A woman's heart," said the agent, and Walter went out and slammed the door.

He had to change a good deal of what he thought about Con. The foolish expenditure, the wasted investments, all of that was wrong. She had used it to buy the house on King Street, to buy back a past that he despised, had hoped to overcome — had, by God, overcome. And he, who could have had it for nothing, had offered to buy it. Connie's white rose.

"Well, anyway," he told himself, "I went to King Street."

There was the dinner, and the show, and the nightclub, and the girl. She wasn't so bad as women went, a little older than the one he'd had in Detroit, was it, or Dallas? A little sadder, more tired, more jaded. She looked like a million dollars though, they all did, with her blond hair puffed up in some extraordinary way he recognized as fashionable. She had a nice apartment, and gave him some really good bourbon. When she changed into a long green dress, a hostess gown he supposed it was, and quite exotic, with gold embroidery, and peculiar sleeves, like wings, or leaves, and with her hair puffed up like that, he thought she looked like a single stalk that had somehow become detached from its proper place in a field of summer corn. The country image sustained him, and he enjoyed himself.

Later, he caught a plane, and went home. He went straight

in to the chief's office, from the airport, and reported on the results of his trip. That took the best part of the morning, but eventually he was able to get to his own desk, and open up his overnight bag. He went next door, where his two secretaries, Peggy and Alice, worked, one on either side of a partition. That had been his own idea, knowing, as he knew, how women were, gossiping all day long. To Peggy, the older, though neither of them were young, he gave the alligator handbag. He hadn't had it wrapped, and for a moment wondered if he had taken the price tag off. But it didn't matter. Everyone knew what alligator handbags cost.

"It's wonderful!" she said, opening and closing it, and holding it up in front of her. "You shouldn't have!"

"I owed you something," said Walter. "Best secretary I ever had." He went on in to Alice, whose continual typing betrayed her as not wanting to seem as though she expected anything. He handed her the package containing the perfume, and she gave a delighted shriek, like a child.

"Perfume," she said, "and the biggest size! What did I ever do to deserve that?"

"Best secretary I ever had," said Walter, lowering his voice so that Peggy, now audibly back to work, would not hear him. "Put me through to my wife, will you." Back at his desk, he picked up the phone.

"Constance?" he said, and caught himself. "Con? I'm home. Yes, a good trip. No time for shopping, I'm afraid." He listened for a moment. "I didn't go near the place. No time. Anyway, someone told me it was all torn down." He listened further to the well-known voice, loved and hated. "Torn down," he repeated. "Urban renewal or something.

You know how they do." The voice went on, and he became angry. "I don't care what you were told," he said. "King Street doesn't exist."

He put down the phone with the feeling that there was still something to be done, something he had forgotten. After a while he remembered, and emptied the ashes in his coat pocket onto a sheet of white paper on his desk. Carefully folding it, he dropped it in the wastebasket.

Irongate

UNLIKE SOME OF THE OTHER inmates, fretting for a large
untidy past, and lost authority, Mrs. Hampden liked being at
the Home. She had laid most careful plans for her retirement
there. New books and records arrived frequently from Har-
rods, and she had her own furniture. The approach of senility
might have seemed something of a comfort to her, the stric-
tures of her sharp censorious mind like a tight corset she would
be glad to take off and put away; as she had indeed put away
actual corsets, and allowed herself to grow quite stout. But it
proved more difficult for Mrs. Hampden to remove herself
from her demanding intelligence than she had expected. A
mind like one of those old-fashioned steamer trunks, said
Winifred, her daughter. Everything that ever happened to her
locked away inside, bound with iron straps, never to be relinquished. All Mrs. Hampden was able to do was to separate
herself from all recollection of her daughter and granddaughter. This she did very successfully, and forgot entirely who
they were. Winifred maintained she had done it out of
perversity, and Caroline was inclined to agree. It was not easy
to understand how one could be quite forgotten, utterly erased

from memory. It seemed to argue that one was dead, or close to it, finished with, the forgetful one more alive than one was oneself.

Mrs. Hampden was old, very old, and sometimes claimed not to know when she had been born, half closing her eyes, trembling, smiling foolishly, acting out of her childhood some ludicrous pantomime of Gaffer Hampden, Oldest Inhabitant. But at other times she rapped out sharply at the other old women, hurling precise recollections at them, like balled-up pages of a memoir she had decided not to publish, dross of her life, as they doddered about the lounge with a copy of *House and Garden*, looking for a lost pair of glasses, a misplaced knitting needle. Despising her companions, who knitted woollies for themselves and each other, shapeless affairs of the finest yarn in the dullest possible colors, Mrs. Hampden said when she was a girl she had a dress with a bustle, of striped black-and-yellow silk — she must have looked, quite suitably, like a wasp, thought the others — and had been in London when Queen Victoria died, and watched the funeral procession from a window in Whitehall. Several of the other women had traveled, remembered years in India, and in Africa, but everything they had done seemed pale in comparison to what Mrs. Hampden stated rather than boasted of, as their woollies and the art that composed them seemed inane, pointless, even a little vulgar, compared with Mrs. Hampden's embroidery. Astonishingly clear-sighted for her age, she did fine stitching on an endless series of linens. Sheets and pillowcases, tablecloths and hand towels, lilac on purple, crimson on pink, gray on white, which the nurses sent to the laundry to be washed and starched, and regretfully put away in an enormous trunk in the basement, labeled *Mrs. Hampden's Belongings.* Except for Miss Beacon, the youngest but not at all youthful nurse, engaged to be married, and filling her hope chest. She had quite a quantity of Mrs. Hampden's embroidered sheets and pillowcases, neatly folded in her own narrow closet. Not exactly a theft, but a simple abstraction of what would never be missed. Such quality would never be repeated. Miss Beacon had a real fondness for Mrs. Hampden, and a great admiration for what was handmade. She was waiting for Mrs. Hampden to finish a set of a dozen napkins and a tablecloth, hoping the work would be accomplished before November, when she would hand in her resignation.

Alone in her room, Mrs. Hampden gave in completely to being old. At night she sat on the edge of her bed, and cut at her corns with a little razor sheathed in mother-of-pearl, raising her mottled foot to rest upon her mottled knee. She smelled faintly of wintergreen and camphor, and talked to herself in vicious tones as she scraped at her aged skin. She had been a beauty, married young, and was disappointed. She'd had a child, but not liked it much, a great slobbering baby, held it far from her, at arm's length from her laced and ribboned batiste bodices, not caring for its lack of control and the disagreeable consequences thereof. Good-natured, but not good-tempered, she had flourished in the golden years of the last century, waited during the next three decades for something tremendous to happen to her, and withered away bit by bit, ripening, spoiling, as nothing more momentous occurred than assassinations, wars, and shocking change in the order of the universe. The baby grew up, tottered about on the lawn at Ridgely, in layers of starched cotton, a large hat with a feather, and a wide pink sash. Eventually ran off and got married to an unsuitable man. Mrs. Hampden took her own first steps toward being what she now was — old, embittered, tyrannical.

Upright in the dining room, whenever she chose to dine there, she ruled the table she sat at, as the wealthy woman she was, who had endowed the place, insisted on her own program, her own menu, cauliflower au gratin and macaroni cheese banished forever, together with heated-up tinned fish, whose unsavory odors she may have detected on her first tour of inspection. Otherwise, how could she ever have known of the existence of such humble dishes? She had had the front gates installed when she moved there, and given the Home its name — Irongate.

·

The gates shut out the town, crowded, as Mrs. Hampden surmised with a certain accuracy, with old people, waiting for vacancies in the nursing homes, of which Irongate was one. Shut out her past life, having to be unlocked before Winifred and Caroline could be admitted, they the only relics of her life before her arrival at Irongate. They drove down dutifully three times a year, rarely enough, and then only to impress the nurses, salve their consciences, and make their small, ineffectual efforts to regain the gates. Mrs. Hampden's tongue and temper being what they were, neither Winifred nor Caroline looked forward to the moment when — Caroline driving ever more slowly — they must arrive outside Irongate. But they enjoyed the long drive, took care to arrange their visits to coincide with the happiest moments of the countryside. They went in October, when the beeches were blazing, and the roads slippery with wet leaves, a smell of cider rising from the orchards. Again, in spring, and exclaimed to each other over the wildflowers, heartsease and cowslip; and the new lambs bounding. And then in high summer, brown and white cows beneath the willows, cornfields strewn with poppies.

For several miles before they reached Briholme, the cliffs were crowded with trailer camps, tents, flapping lines of wet bathing suits, and a running, shrieking voices-lost-in-the-wind population of young families, more of them this summer than ever before. Winifred and Caroline had expected the worst, but it seemed as they drove into the town that Briholme was still regarded as sacrosanct, sedate and quiet, the refuge of the old. Flowers in baskets were strung on the light standards of the main street. The little park was bedded out with foreign-looking plants, all in full bloom, scarlet and intense blue, white and hot pink. Looming over the bandstand, a statue of Nelson faced the wrong way, landward, a seagull perched on his shoulder. On the Esplanade, old people tottered, two by two. The beach was empty, but the cliff paths were scattered with cripples and the blind, arms linked with watchful, uniformed duennas. On one of the benches, looking out to sea, sat a group of parents of hydrocephalic children, beside the specially constructed, wheeled containers for their young, who gurgled and babbled and nodded their vast heads, and kicked their patent-leather shoes against the wicker of their basket chairs. Everyone in Briholme, thought Caroline, seemed to be the victim of some awful accident, in space, in time, or in the genes.

On the other side of the town, past the shops, The Copper Kettle teashop, and the Palm Gardens Hotel — where the bored and heat-exhausted doorman straightened hopefully at the approach of Caroline's little Austin, subsided disappointedly as she drove on — past the little crescent of houses built in the time of the Prince Regent, stood the cliff-top nursing homes.

"Fernleigh, Rosemont," said Caroline, reading the signs growing out of clumps of hydrangea and valerian. "Primrose Court. It's further on."

"Gunnydale Hall," said Winifred. She sat very upright, as women in their sixties who have kept their figures, remained slender, tend to do, denying age. Her rather smart straw hat was placed quite straight on her head, and her gloved hands were clasped precisely over a paperback book in her lap.

"Oh, Mother," said Caroline. "Sunnydale. You ought to wear glasses."

"There's nothing wrong with my sight," said Winifred. They had had that argument before, as indeed they had had every argument before. "It's that gothic lettering." There was a great deal of gothic lettering in Briholme. The Copper Kettle and the Palm Gardens Hotel had menus printed in it, almost every sign and direction was designed to be deciphered rather than read. Caroline wondered if the local newspaper went in for it much. "Here it is, Irongate," said Winifred, and Caroline slowed down, stopped, and pulled on the brake. She ran her fingers through her short hair, black turning to gray, damp in Briholme's peculiar sluggish heat, curl fallen out. She leaned her elbow on the open window of the car, and lighted a cigarette.

"You might give me one too," said Winifred.

"Oh, sorry, Mother. I'd forgotten you'd given up giving it up."

"Sarcasm is unbecoming in women," said Winifred, accepting a cigarette from the proffered packet. She blew smoke through her nostrils, looked for a moment like a portrait of a horse, tapped the ash into the ashtray. "It sharpens the features." Caroline looked at her in amused exasperation. Her mother was an Edwardian at heart, as nonchalantly daring in her smoking as when she was a girl, subscribing still to outmoded rules of conduct. Both women turned their attention to the gates. Eighteenth-century, beautifully and fantastically wrought, a design of iron fruits and flowers was surmounted by a tremendous letter R, and a curious animal, lioness or leopard. Built to allow the passage of a great family coach — and locked. Winifred could hardly recall a time when they were not. In early youth she had been locked in, and, as soon as she got away, she was locked out. Now, it was a condition of the endowment. Mrs. Hampden's whim, said one of the cleverer nurses, waiting impatiently for the latest in a succession of unsatisfactory gatemen to allow her entrances and exits to the nursing home.

The posts which had originally supported the gates stood miles away, outside Winifred's house on the old Ridgely estate. Caroline wished her mother would take them down, had never put them up, such ostentatiousness, such a proclaiming that she had rights at Ridgely that dated from very long before, before the time of the red-brick houses of the new suburb, before Ridgely Garden City. The gateposts, though, and the gates were all that was left of the old Ridgely. Everything else was gone, the lawns where Winifred had ridden her pony, the driveway beneath the elms where she had walked with that charming man, her music teacher, later and briefly her husband. Now there was a new road, constant building, uprooting, tearing and gouging. On Sundays the bulldozers lay drawn up against the grass verges like sleeping dragons.

.

"Well," said Winifred. "It must be two o'clock. Oughtn't we to be moving on?" Caroline threw away her cigarette, got out of the car, walked up to the gates and rang the bell. The gateman appeared, a young man this time, with a shock of black hair and an impudent expression. He sauntered to the gates, unlocked and opened them. "Silly, isn't it?" he said, as Caroline got back in the driver's seat. "Makes trouble for you and makes trouble for me. But there it is. That's the way it has to be." Caroline tried to give him some sort of a salute as she drove past, but she was on the wrong side, and was faintly annoyed to see how he responded, almost bowing, though ironically, to Winifred's unsmiling nod.

"You look like the queen," she said crossly, and changed into second out of a kind of reckless irritation. The car faltered and coughed, and she had to change down again.

"Why not?" said Winifred. "Really well-bred people can't help but emulate the royal family. Their good manners . . . Why don't you put on your gloves, Caroline? You should never drive without them."

"Here?" said Caroline. The car wasn't going to make the hill. "And in this weather?" She was again amused, again annoyed, to see how it worked. Always the same. Scratch the royal family, and you find a pair of white gloves.

"Perhaps you'd better put on the brake, and start again

from the beginning," said Winifred, much as an early school-mistress had told Caroline to practice her scales. "No, no, no! Start again, from the beginning." She'd been supposed to have been born with music in her blood, but as a matter of fact had neither ear nor interest.

"She can do it," said Caroline, obstinately, feeling middle-aged and henpecked, gloveless and untidy, but suddenly determined that she wouldn't take another suggestion, or pick up another hint, or say another word. And she did, the little Austin, soaring obediently to the top of the hill just as Caroline had given up hope, pausing quietly and triumphantly beneath the portico.

"Hooray!" called the young man with the black hair, who had watched the whole operation with interest. He waved his arm. Caroline waved back. This time Winifred paid no attention. The exuberance of the public had gone too far.

"Now, do tell her about the gates," she said. "Make it clear, if you can, that I came too, down from Ridgely, I mean, but that I have a slight headache, and I won't be seeing her." Caroline looked at her, shocked.

"You won't?"

"Not this time. Last time, she had me mixed up with Judith, and your father was Holofernes. I can't think why. So military, and your father wasn't at all like that." Caroline sat musing in the sunshine, looking at her mother with narrowed eyes and pursed lips. Judith. So unlike, what a strange obsession. Who could have been less passionately partisan than Winifred? "She held up a head," Winifred went on. "Dripping with blood. Not really, of course. A pineapple from a bowl of fruit. But just the same. It was embarrassing and painful. I don't want to go through it again. And I've brought a book." She patted the paperback she held in her lap. "Don't worry about me."

"But wouldn't you rather wait in the hall?" said Caroline. "One of the nurses would probably bring you some tea. Or take a little walk? The rose gardens. They seem to have plenty of roses. You like roses, don't you?"

"Actually, not very," said Winifred. She settled her hat more firmly on her brow, riffled through the pages of her book. "It's rather nouveau, don't you think, all this recent interest in roses?" At Ridgely Garden City, roses were grown with enthusiasm, responded in kind. Everyone was an expert on hybrid teas. Winifred knew only two. Phillis Bide, and Climbing Albertine.

Caroline sighed, and left her. She rang the bell beside the nail-studded door, as gothic as the lettering common in Briholme. After a moment it was opened. A uniformed nurse stood there.

"Oh dear," she said. "I thought you were the bus."

"I've come to see Mrs. Hampden," said Caroline. "I'm her granddaughter."

"Mrs. Hampden, of course. Well, you see, I thought you were the bus. We're all going to the zoo today, and it's ten minutes late. Do come inside." The hall was cool and dark. On a Jacobean chest a spray of fuchsia wept over a pile of motoring magazines.

"I hope I won't be keeping my grandmother from going to the zoo," said Caroline. It sounded ludicrous.

"Oh, no. Not Mrs. Hampden. She wouldn't go in any case. I'm Miss Beacon, by the way."

"How do you do?" said Caroline.

"I don't think I was here when you came before. I haven't been here very long. Last, but not least, as Matron says."

"She wouldn't go to the zoo? Why not?"

"Well, she has a different program. She's on a different schedule from the others. Her own wavelength, you might say."

"Of course," said Caroline, remembering some of her grandmother's curious regulations for herself. Music, books, meals in her room if she wanted them. She'd never known how far it went. Evidently, quite far. Everyone else to be herded and shepherded, but not she. "I'd forgotten. She has things very nicely arranged for herself."

"Some might say so," said Miss Beacon. "But then again, this isn't like some places I could mention." Her eyes went from left to right, as though she were seeing and condemning through the walls certain practices at Sunnydale Hall, Primrose Court and Fernleigh. "There's always something going on. A birthday party, a picnic, bingo games. And today we're going to the zoo. But there's some who don't care to participate, and in my opinion it's their loss."

"I'm sure it is," said Caroline, feeling some comfort was needed.

"If you'll just follow me . . . They're all so impatient, sweet old things, they do so love an outing." Caroline followed her out of the hall and into a sun-filled conservatory, where a number of elderly women sat in an orderly row in brightly painted summer chairs. They were all wearing hats, of varying degrees of eccentricity, and their ancient legs, whether heavily stout or pitifully thin, were all encased in elastic bandages under their stockings, all ended in orthopedic shoes.

"We won't be long now," said Miss Beacon cheerfully. "Just a few minutes, and we'll all be off."

"It's a shame," said someone wrathfully. "The way they keep us waiting. No consideration."

"A picnic? Is it a picnic?" asked the old lady nearest them. "I didn't make any sandwiches, you know."

"Silly old fool," said the one who had first spoken.

"Not this time," said Miss Beacon. "Not a picnic, this time. This time, it's the zoo. Won't that be nice?"

"Will we see the bears?" said the anxious old lady. "They like sugar lumps. I haven't got any sugar lumps."

"They'll give them to you on the bus," said Miss Beacon. "Don't worry."

"Sugar lumps?" said the angry one. "Sugar lumps for *bears*? Currant buns are what bears like best." Miss Beacon disengaged her sleeve from the tremulous old fingers.

"Wonderful, the interest they take, isn't it?" she said, leading the way back to the hall.

"Wonderful," said Caroline, although she felt dubious.

"It's healthy," said the nurse aggressively, as though she somehow sensed Caroline's doubt. "If they don't, they just — " She glanced over her shoulder at the row of old women, lowered her voice. "*Pass over*."

"I see." Looking back at the old women, she felt she did see. There came a time — Ah, but when? — when life was too much, had to be narrowed down to a single event. A single dish at a particular meal, a stitch saved from falling off a needle full of a row of them, a visit to the zoo.

"There wouldn't be much satisfaction in a job like this," said the nurse, regarding her charges with some complacency, "if they were all like Mrs. Hampden."

"Not everyone enjoys group activities," suggested Caroline, though timidly. They went down a corridor, and paused before a closed door.

"They miss a lot, when they don't," said Miss Beacon, and opened the door.

Something Victorian about the room, flowered wallpaper, damask curtains, a curly mahogany chest, and a heavy framed mirror. Caroline always forgot there would be none of the chintz and nubby linen she glimpsed in other rooms. A combination hi-fi, radio and television glared at her balefully from a corner with its many-buttoned eyes. Peppermints in a glass dish and a row of medicine bottles stood on the night table. Mrs. Hampden sat by the window, with a view of the gravel drive, a corner of the rose garden, and, if she craned her neck through the open window, a view of the sea, through the cedars and pines. She was reading a book as they came in. Caroline had the impression that she had begun to doze over it.

"We have a visitor," said the nurse, with a sudden coyness. "Isn't that nice? Not to stay long, mind. We don't want that nasty blood pressure going up, do we? Doctor would give us a fearful talking-to, if we let that happen."

"He wouldn't give *us* a talking-to, as you call it," said Mrs. Hampden, coming awake suddenly and completely. She closed the book she was holding, *The Life of Charles Darwin.* "He'd be afraid of our having a stroke. He might give you one. You might get fired. That's what we have to be careful of."

"Naughty, naughty," said the nurse, and quite unnecessarily, for the room was warm, picked up a shawl that had fallen to the floor, and draped it about Mrs. Hampden's shoulders. She removed the book and placed it on the night table, clicking her tongue. "Spoiling our eyes," she scolded. "How are we going to get our embroidery done, if we do that?" She smiled at Caroline. "Can't have that, can we?" she said. Her tone was infectious, though her use of pronouns unclear.

"No, indeed," said Caroline, her tone full of false raillery, uncertain as to whether she might not add something else. But the vocabulary seemed to be limited. Naughty, naughty. Come now. This won't do. "Oh, Grandmother," she said, in relief, as the door closed behind the nurse. "How are you?" She sank into a chair opposite the old lady.

"They'll bring us some tea in a moment," said Mrs. Hampden. She shook the shawl off her shoulders. It fell to the floor exactly as it had been before. "They do you quite well here. It would be like a rather superior hotel, if it weren't for the distinctly inferior clientele."

"They are taking care of you?" said Caroline. "Everything's all right, isn't it?"

"Certainly," said her grandmother. "Kind of you to ask, of course. What are you? One of those women with a fountain pen and a sheaf of papers and a mission? Collecting statistics as girls used to gather wildflowers? I understand there's a lot of that, nowadays."

"No," said Caroline. "No. I'm . . . Caroline. Your granddaughter."

"There's no such thing," said Mrs. Hampden, "as a grown-up granddaughter. Indeed, you look positively middle-aged.

I'm sorry to say it, but I mean it kindly. Couldn't you do something about your hair? You seem to have no — no *coiffure*. Or none to speak of." Caroline's hand went to her untidy, careless locks, as her grandmother went on. "Granddaughters are little and small, they cluster about one's knees. Surely you know that?" She spoke fiercely, pinned Caroline down with eyes like blue daisies, framed in startled-looking pale lashes.

"Well, I was," said Caroline, defensively, smoothing her hair and bringing her hand down again. "Little and small, I mean. But I've grown. I can't help that. I'm still related to you."

"Are you indeed?" Mrs. Hampden regarded Caroline reflectively. "Well, I can't help *that*," she said. "Here's tea." A maid in a striped pinafore brought in a tray, and set it down on the dressing table. A pot of tea, two cups, a plate of biscuits.

"No, no, no," said Mrs. Hampden. "On the tea table. Here. How many times . . . ?" To Caroline, as the maid effected the change, she said in a low voice, "Impossible to get good help, nowadays. These girls . . ."

She still thinks she's running her own home, thought Caroline. Poor thing. Aloud, she said, "Shall I pour?"

"If you would," said Mrs. Hampden. "Age puts one under many obligations. I've got very stiff, I'm afraid. Not to pour one's own tea in one's own room. A lesser ill, I suppose. Who did you say you were?"

"Caroline." Handed her a cup of tea, two biscuits poised in the saucer.

"Caroline. Odd, isn't it, how the old names have come back? Winifred, Edith, Maud. Caroline, Harriet, Annabel.

But you came to tell me something. Drink your tea." She looked down at her saucer. "I'll have to speak to them. They never bring me the biscuits with icing on them. They know I like those best."

"I came to ask you something," said Caroline, boldly. "The gates, Grandmother."

Years before, she had known about them. Her mother had settled in the gamekeeper's cottage, at the edge of the estate, and called it the Dower House. Caroline was brought up there. Out for a walk, in her teens, pushing through the thickets of overgrown rhododendron, she had discovered Ridgely, burned down before she was born. A flight of marble stairs, broken off short. A faun, drinking from a shattered cup, a series of rooms, outlined with walls only a foot or two high, carpeted in anemone and periwinkle. She had never seen Ridgely itself, glimmering through the trees, that lovely house at the end of the curving driveway. Ridgely Hall, More Glass Than Wall, was what the country people said, when it was first built. Ridgelys had lived there from the early eighteenth century. They had some connections at court. A cousin, Thomas Ball, rakish, a great dandy, "Ornamental" Ball, he was called, a boon companion of the Prince Regent. He played cards disastrously, married a Ridgely daughter and wagered her away. There was a scandal. Someone had been shot with a pearl-handled pistol. Ridgely was full of legend. Caroline, adolescent, stumbled on the gateposts at the edge of the woods, one standing upright still, a sentinel grown over with moss and wound about with ivy, the other lying prone in the weeds. The gates themselves were gone.

"Mother has them," said Winifred later. "They were just about the only things left, after the fire. Heaven knows why she sets such store by them. But she's like that. Very contrary. So determined that I shouldn't have anything. She'd have taken the Dower House, if it could have been moved. If Father hadn't left it to me."

Winifred had woven a myth about herself, a fantastic tissue of fact and fancy, and Caroline early ceased to believe in the tale of her mother as a disinherited princess, and thought that to run off with a piano teacher, no matter how sweetly he played, was a stupid thing to have done. That act of Edwardian folly had put Winifred outside the gates of Ridgely forever. Mrs. Hampden never forgave her, became, if anything, more bitter than before, when the piano teacher, having fathered Caroline, ran off for a second time. This time with an heiress who, unlike Winifred, had her own hands firmly on her fortune, and who arranged her elopement with style and at considerable expense. Hotel suites were reserved beforehand all over Europe.

There was Ridgely money for Winifred, but doled out gradually, bit by bit, in a way designed to prevent an extravagant and irresponsible woman from ever really enjoying her vices. The whole story, told over and over by her mother, bored Caroline. She had read travelogues with more interest, novels with better plots. But, in the green shade beneath the rhododendron and the laurel, the statue of the faun shining whitely, she believed for a moment in Ridgely. It had existed, then. After that, she insisted on the visits to Briholme, which Winifred had thought scarcely worth embarking upon.

"The gates?" said Mrs. Hampden now, sipping tea, scattering biscuit crumbs over her tightly buttoned Victorian front. "What gates?" A shadow darkened the window, she turned her head. "The bus. They're all going to the zoo, poor things. There's nothing there, you know. What could Briholme have? I went, once. A disreputable-looking red deer. One of the few remaining in existence, I suppose. A pair of wolves. It is hard to believe that those animals once ranged all over England quite freely. Our history books tell us they did, so I suppose we must believe it. I refuse to go and look at them. Dispossessed. Locked in cages." There were voices in the hall outside, as the old ladies prepared to board the bus. Shuffling footsteps, a childlike excitement.

"Things have changed," said Caroline. "Ridgely is all built over, now, you know."

"Built over?"

"Rows of houses. A shopping center. A bank. They call it Ridgely Garden City."

"A *bank?* At Ridgely?" Caroline nodded. "Nice houses?" Mrs. Hampden sounded a little uncertain. Caroline hesitated.

"Very convenient," she said. "Small, of course. And they all look rather alike. That's the thing, you see. Some people have put up little brick walls. Others have planted hedges, privet, and things like that. They try to make them as different as they can. Paint the doors and shutters in different colors."

"Painted doors and shutters?" said Mrs. Hampden. "It sounds charming. Swiss." Caroline considered this, smiled a little.

"Well, yes," she said. "Though the effect is not the same. In any case, Mother's case is different. She has the Dower House. It looks unique enough in itself, you know, the thatch, and those tiny little windows, though it's awfully close to the other houses. She's put up the gateposts from Ridgely."

"Mother?" The old lady put down her teacup and saucer, hand trembling. "No more biscuits?" she said. "They never bring enough."

"I'm afraid not," said Caroline. "Winifred," she added.

"Winifred . . ." Quite flatly, not even a question.

"Your daughter."

"Yes. So you have a mother too, have you?" She moved her blue daisy eyes from Caroline, and looked out of the window. The bus left, spraying gravel. "There never was a Dower House at Ridgely," she said. "It was the game-keeper's cottage. Large, and commodious, considering. But still . . . The gamekeeper's cottage. Ridgely all built over," she went on. "It is difficult to believe. Impossible to imag-ine. And I still don't understand quite . . ."

"What I've come for? The gates. Winifred wants the gates."

"Well, that's very simply disposed of," said Mrs. Hampden, with relief. She gave a short laugh. "She must try Torness, when I've gone. Whoever she may be."

"Torness?"

"The cemetery there. It's where I am to be buried. I've bequeathed the gates to them. It's all in my will. I've made a will, naturally. Some of the women here refuse to do that, you know. But I say death will come no faster, for the sen-sible disposal of one's property."

"But one should be quite sure," said Caroline, "that it *is* sensible."

"Oh, I have no doubts about that," said Mrs. Hampden.

"I have no cat nor kit. I think," she added suddenly, "that Miss Beacon is coming back. My hearing is still fairly acute, and I seem to have developed an extra sense regarding her. I always know when she's on the move. She steals my sheets . . ."

"Had a nice tea?" said Miss Beacon, opening the door, popping her head in, and speaking, all at once. "What a naughty thing we are, we finished all the biscuits. It'll be on a diet for us, young lady." She collected plates busily, replaced Mrs. Hampden's shawl. "I think she's had enough, now," she said under her breath to Caroline. "Did she go on about her will?" Caroline nodded. "That's never a good sign."

"I suppose you have to leave now," said Mrs. Hampden, "Miss . . ."

"Caroline." She stood up, straightened her skirt.

"Caroline. Odd, isn't it, how the old names have come back. What's *your* name?" She turned to the nurse.

"My first name? Ah, that'd be telling, wouldn't it? But in confidence, mind, it's Marilyn."

"What kind of a name is that?" said Mrs. Hampden, frowning, wrinkling her brow. "Well, never mind. I expect there'll be a place for you."

"At Torness?" said Caroline wickedly. She opened her handbag, consulted a mirror, and took out her gloves, began pulling them on.

"At Torness? What are you talking about? Oh, dear no, I shouldn't think so. Torness is reserved for people of substance. A good deal of the wealth of England is gathered in this small corner of it, you know." Her eyes, seeming to twinkle, though perhaps it was only rheum, caught Caroline's hands. "I'm so glad to see you wearing gloves. Young women, nowadays . . . But of course, you are no longer . . . A woman of a certain age, rather." She nodded to herself, seemed almost to doze off.

"I really must go," said Caroline, in response to violent signals from the nurse.

"Of course, one can't tell," said Mrs. Hampden, opening her remarkable eyes, and looking penetratingly at Miss Beacon. "Perseverance and an acquisitive nature may work wonders."

"Well, I'll have to be off," said Caroline.

"Do come again," said Mrs. Hampden. "I've enjoyed our little chat, Miss — "

"Caroline."

"Yes, of course. Odd, isn't it, how the old names . . . ?" Caroline left her, as the nurse turned on the record player, and the notes of Scarlatti filled the air. She was followed by them through the hall, past the weeping spray of fuchsia, and out to the car, where her mother sat and read a detective story by Agatha Christie.

"No use," she said. Winifred closed her book.

"No use?"

"None. She didn't know me, of course. I'm afraid her mind is really going. She said something about the nurse stealing her sheets."

"Right off her bed? That can't be," said Winifred, shocked.

"She was talking nonsense, of course. The nurse isn't that sort. Rather sweet, I thought, considering."

"And the gates?"

"She's leaving them to the cemetery at Torness, when she dies."

"Taking them with her to the bitter end," said Winifred bleakly. "No family sense. She was always like that. Very contrary."

The car spluttered and started reluctantly. "Still, I'm a little sorry for her. Old people's homes are rather dreadful places. Did you see all the old ladies going off on some excursion on the bus? And the bus driver was older than they were. I'd be surprised if they got safely to wherever they were going."

"The zoo," said Caroline tiredly. "They were going to look at the red deer."

"It's extinct," said Winifred. "I'm almost sure it is. Perhaps they were going to see a stuffed one." She shivered. "Dreadful, dreadful. What a fate."

"We'll probably end up here ourselves," said Caroline, not believing it. The car didn't like the steep slope down to the gates, slid a little. She thought she must really get the brakes relined. Winifred looked at her in horror.

"What an awful thing to say! Don't speak of such frightful things!"

The gateman, condition of the endowment, subdued now in the late afternoon, his shock of black hair less showy, came out of his house and unlocked the gates for them. Caroline, on the correct side this time, smiled at him, and felt suddenly deeply gratified when he smiled back. But his attention was really on the car.

"Needs a thorough overhaul and a tune-up, shouldn't be surprised," he said. "Never thought you'd make it, going up *or* coming down. Bang into them gates, I thought, and then won't all the old biddies be in a taking. Have a proper fit. Be the death of some of 'em, shouldn't wonder."

As they turned into the road, and started back to the main street of Briholme, Winifred clicked her tongue.

"Give them an inch, and they'll take an ell," she said. "Smile politely, and they think they've made a lifelong friend."

"I suppose I should have the car seen to," said Caroline. "I don't think we ought to go back tonight. We'd better make a long weekend of it, and stay overnight in Briholme."

So they stayed at the Palm Gardens Hotel, refuge of the very old, of elderly ladies awaiting admittance to Primrose Court, Sunnydale Hall, Irongate.

At the Lake

THEY CAME OUT of the hotel to a wet morning, the long weekend already a third gone, not quite sure of what to do next. The rain hung like fine silent needles, a curtain of silver threads connecting earth and sky. Across the street a shopkeeper slowly unfurled a green-and-white-striped awning over his window. The legend Johnson and Johnson, Fine Jewels, inscribed in a giant schoolboy hand, became visible. Sophie and Alec looked skyward. The unfurling of the awning was a testimony of faith, a belief that the weather would clear up. It was summer, after all.

The shop window twinkled and glittered with diamonds, watches, and cut-glass bowls. Sophie took a triangle of plastic, patterned to look like lace, out of her pocket, and tied it over her hair.

"Let's take a look in there," said Alec Forbush, and they crossed the street as Johnson vanished into the interior of his shop.

There were cameras and projectors at one side of the display. She might have known. They stood together in silence, not altogether companionable, frowning into the collection of objects, she glancing quickly from ring to ring, each in its satin-lined box, fine bargains at fifty-eight pounds; rapidly untangling with her eyes the little heap of old-fashioned things, amethyst and turquoise, lockets set with seed pearls, gold chains spilling over the edge of a painted fruit plate, and he musing over the Rolleiflex and the light meters. They were hailed from behind, and both started guiltily, turning like criminals from the window, as though they had been contemplating a theft. A youngish man, a crest of reddish hair, a smile of pure malice.

"Well, well, well," he said. "What a surprise. One never knows who one might run into, does one?"

"One certainly doesn't," said Alec Forbush, after a moment. "And in point of fact, I'm afraid I've forgotten your name."

"Brackenridge," said the youngish man. "Ted Brackenridge. You know me. I'm on your building committee. I thought it was you when I saw you cross the street. And this is my wife." A woman with a simper, a tweed suit, reddish hair to match her husband's had detached herself from the small car parked at the curb, and appeared at Brackenridge's elbow.

"Mrs. Brackenridge," said Alec. "How do you do?" He made no attempt to introduce Sophie, but took her by the elbow aggressively, as though he were about to hurry her away. "I'm afraid we've got to be going," he said, as Brackenridge smiled again and peered into the jeweler's window.

"What did you find?" he asked. "Anything worthwhile? Sometimes in these country places one comes across the most delightful — " His eyes went swiftly over the rings and watches, paused at the set of enameled spoons with the picture of the cathedral in the bowl. "Now those," he said. "But made in Western Germany, I expect. Nice little town, isn't it?" He gestured toward the hotel Alec and Sophie had just left. "We're staying over there. Do you have any idea of what it's like?" His smile grew broader and broader.

"Very nice," said Alec. "But we really do have to rush." By this time he was speaking over his shoulder.

"Good-bye, nice to have seen you," said Brackenridge, and his wife simpered.

"It was bound to happen," said Alec, his hand still on Sophie's arm, urging her down the street. "I daresay there isn't a town in England, probably not a town on the continent, where we wouldn't have run into Brackenridge, or somebody like him." Guiding her down the street, toward the car.

"I'm awfully sorry," said Sophie, guiltless, quite calm. It had happened before. "I thought you carried it off very well." She stood waiting demurely in the rain that beat down gently on her plastic hood, while he unlocked the car door.

They were parked in the shadow of the cathedral. Above them, the square tower vanished into fog. The iron chain railings of the close glistened with wet. Toward the river the trees became strange bosomy shapes, mistily described. The night before they had walked beside the river, thrown pennies from the bridge, watched the geese. This morning you couldn't see anything of that.

"Of course he'll see my name in the register," said Alec. He held the door for her. "I don't know which is worse. That, or seeing us gawking over engagement rings."

"Perhaps the effect of one will cancel out the other," said

Sophie. "Perhaps he'll think we're going to be married." It amused her sometimes to give him little alarms.

"Oh, I don't think so," said Alec, getting in beside her. "He's very worldly, is Brackenridge. Not that I know him. On my building committee, he said. He must sit at the far end of the table. But you can tell."

"So he won't do anything," said Sophie. Alec shrugged.

"It depends. He might. There's probably someone on the board who's in charge of things like this. But it won't matter. I'm too valuable for it to matter."

"I hope I am too," said Sophie, gently.

"Why? You didn't know him, did you?" She shook her head.

"No. No, I'm the mysterious Madame X, so far as he's concerned."

"Then that's all right then." He gave a distracted look about the interior of the car, at their two small suitcases on the back seat, took his camera from around his neck. "Have we *got* everything?" he asked. "Is there anything left out? I almost always leave a pair of socks under the bed, or my pajama top in the bathroom."

"I checked everything," said Sophie.

"Well then. Shall we go? Or do you want to go round the cathedral? See it properly?" She hesitated. They had seen something of it the evening before, heard evensong, admired the Perpendicular dark choir and the Norman font, seen the tracery in the cloisters. And she had bought two sepia-tinted postcards — she couldn't send them to anyone, since no one was supposed to know where she was — while a bishop was being inducted, led down the aisle to the altar, palms upturned. Somewhere there was a Saxon grave, that of the Atheling, or one of the Ethelreds, robbed long ago, nothing left but a grassy mound in the graveyard, and a marker put up by the Historical Graves Association. Perhaps, deep down, a finger bone, and the pattern of a jeweled sword, impressed in the clay.

"I believe I've had enough of Westford," she said.

"Good enough," said Alec, and began to back and turn in the narrow space. "A pretty wife, I thought," he said, as he struggled with the wheel.

"Oh, yes, very pretty," said Sophie, and thought, not for the first time, that he had no taste, and what would he have said if she had started raving about Brackenridge?

They got out of the parking space, came to the town square, crowded with tractors, reaping machines, and threshers, the rain shining on their blue and red and yellow sides, where a policeman in a shiny black cape directed traffic, waved them genially but implacably on to the north, whether they wanted to go there or not.

"Where shall we go?" said Alec, driving fast in the rain that obscured the side windows, silver nails dotting the glass. Sophie sighed. A woman would have drawn to the side of the road, consulted a map, discussed it thoroughly.

"I don't know," she said. "Wherever you like." There was silence for a few minutes. A hay wain loomed up ahead of them, horsedrawn. Her heart came up into her mouth, but Alec negotiated it successfully.

"The lake, then?" he said.

"Oh, yes. I'd love to."

And suddenly, as though it were a signal, his suggestion, her

ready agreement, the rain stopped, they drove out of the
downpour into clear sunlight, a washed world, the road
sparkling ahead of them, the fields green and shining, a pony
galloping, and a woman carrying a basket of laundry into a
cottage garden where hollyhocks sprang upright, released of
their burden of water by her rough passing.

"All right. To the lake," said Alec. "There you are. I
knew the weather would change. We might even swim
there." His hand groped through the maps and guidebooks
lying on the seat between them, found her fingers and
covered them. She returned the pressure and smiled.

.

And so they went to the lake, hurrying away from everything
that had gone wrong and delayed them. Clive, her husband,
going to Geneva a day late; one of Alec's children coming
down with an inflamed throat, and having to be brought
home from camp; Letty's cable from Monaco, she wanted to
discuss a divorce. And that opened vast possibilities to be
hashed over between the two of them, if Alec had wanted to
talk about it, but it seemed that he didn't. And Mary,
Sophie's daughter, said her bearded young man from the
Slade School wanted to marry her, and had insisted on going
to Brussels with him to find out if he were worth living with.

"But *Brussels*, darling," said Sophie. "How can you find
out anything about a person there? Isn't there some other
place, more suitable to prehoneymoon meditation?" She
meant a mountain, a seashore, a river. Of course they were
sleeping together. But in Brussels! A dingy network of dirty
streets and railways. It had all been ironed out. Letty was

put off for a week. (Sophie would have liked to know what Alec said to her, but he didn't tell her.) Clive had packed and gone, catching the plane in the nick of time, with all the brouhaha and last-minute rushing of secretaries and aides that accompanied his most casual movements. Roddie was given antibiotics and sent back to camp in time for the sports events. Mary and her bearded young man decided on a barge trip through Holland instead, Mary amply forewarned, armed with money, told to come to her mother whatever the problem, to marry or not, just as she pleased, these things can always be worked out somehow, though a bride always looks nicest in white, and Clive would enjoy a big wedding. What *could* you say to a girl who might have an illegitimate baby any minute? Still, you had to let them lead their own lives.

Even so, everything that could possibly go wrong had done so. They drove up from London in bad weather, the castle they wanted to visit was closed for repairs, the phrase BAN THE BOMB slashed in whitewash along the west wall. The country pubs they stopped at were crowded with motorcyclists in black leather jackets, engaged in noisy, elliptical conversation and threatening games with the owners. Westford, when they came to it, celebrating an agricultural fair, the hotel full, the bathroom down the hall.

And the night. She preferred not to think about the night.

"Oh, yes," she said again. "I'd love to go to the lake."

They had been lovers for several years, eight or nine, they professed not to know exactly, but long enough for habit to take on the appearance of respectability, at least as far as they were concerned. They believed their curious double life, which had fitted in so well with the frequent absences and general absent-mindedness of their spouses, was the concern of no one but each other. Possibly it would not have held much interest for either Clive or Letty, busy as they were with the making and spending of money. Not that Alec or Sophie claimed to be in love. They rarely mentioned the word. They admitted only to having "a thing" about each other, not understanding that by this they meant they *had* fallen in love, fallen in love with a passion, and a passion that endured, despite — perhaps because of — the urgent moments snatched in little hotels, in the upper rooms of shady restaurants. They had had their one extraordinary experience of romance, sparked somehow on the evening when they met on the terrace of a country house, when they leaned over the balustrade as though on the deck of a ship, and watched two swans on an ornamental pool glide mysteriously through the patch of light cast by the windows. We are those swans, he said, and she thought it an exceedingly profound remark, and treasured it, even to imagining later how the swans would look, out of the water that bore them up. Bedraggled, with soiled feathers and large black feet, spiteful beaks, greedy and ungraceful. He lighted a cigarette for her, and touched her hand with the back of his own, and someone came out through the French doors and called them. Brackenridge was everywhere, even then. What are you two doing? Admiring the moon? There was a moon. They had already gone beyond it, but they looked up, as though noticing the luminous globe for the first time. Letty's looking all over for you, old man, said Brackenridge. I think she wants to go home. She's flipping a fur tippet about as though it were a saber. Oh lord, said Alec, and went. And the Great Man, said Bracken-

ridge, or that early version of him, says he simply must find
his wife and bid his hosts good night. He has to get up early
in the morning. Sophie left too, leaving Brackenridge in pos-
session of the terrace and the moonlight and the swans, thinking resentfully that Clive always had to get up early in the
morning.

It interrupted, but could not prevent, what was to be. A
consummation, after that wildly romantic moment, most
casually achieved, a few weeks later, on a chintz-covered sofa
in the house of a friend of Alec's, out for forty minutes on a
Saturday afternoon in search of cakes for tea. When he came
back they were sitting upright, fully dressed, rather far apart,
listening to Bartók on the radio.

And this morning she had awakened to find an old man in
her bedroom, vigorously brushing his teeth over a washbasin
in the corner, hair on end, eyes flashing over the foaming
toothbrush, and she had wondered, Where am I? And then,
Who am I? Who are we? And remembered the sadness of
the straining night, and turned her face to the pillow. Afterward they had had breakfast together, read the newspapers,
pretended very successfully to be married, and wondered what
they could do on such a wet and uninviting day.

But now the weather had cleared up, they were driving
north, little villages flashed past them.

"I'm looking forward to it," said Sophie. "The lake."

She had never been there, but Alec told her about it.
There were stories of a drowned village, a lost church with
spire intact whose bell had rung in watery warning on the
night of Dunkirk. There were tales of a vast ledge, running
the length of the lake on the north side, dropping off sheer to

unknown depths, and of a great white serpent swimming deep down, its body sinuously undulating around the church tower, its green eyes peering in the windows, where a preacher and his congregation floated forever, birds in a stone cage, weeds growing out of their eye sockets.

"It really isn't a frightfully attractive place," said Alec, as they drove on. "Shut in by the hills, rather heavily wooded on the south shore. And nothing there but a few cottages. But Letty liked it, at one time. She went through a period of wanting to get away from it all."

"What do they do?" said Sophie, ignoring the mention of Letty. "The cottagers? It sounds so lonely."

"Yes, well that's the charm of the place. Its only charm. The remoteness of it. At least we won't run into anyone like Brackenridge there. What do they do? They keep sheep, up on the fells. They fish. They've always been there. It just doesn't occur to them to move."

"But the children. The young people," said Sophie. "Do they like living in a prehistoric slum in the wilds of Cumberland? Don't they have radios, or anything?"

"The boys learn to be shepherds, farmers. The girls knit guernseys for their little brothers in the winter. They make butter, clean fish. One of them cleans the cottage for me, once in a while. I give her five shillings. God knows what she spends it on, or where. I suppose there are copies of the *Housemaids' Weekly* still to be had at the village shop. But I suppose it's a satisfying life, in its way." His foot went down on the accelerator, as though he were anxious to get there.

"It isn't as bad as all that," he said suddenly. "And we have our poet."

"Wordsworth, you mean," said Sophie.

"No, no. I mean, our own poet. Quite a young man. Not a native. Born in Reading, or somewhere like that, as a matter of fact. They call him The Hermit, up there." Sheltered at night in the shepherds' huts, equipped with knotted stick and beard wildly growing, he walked the fells and the valleys, declaiming loudly into the wind.

"Like King Lear," said Sophie.

"Not at all like King Lear. He isn't mad. Just a touch eccentric."

"I'd like to meet him," said Sophie.

"You probably won't," said Alec. "We're all very private, at the lake. Or will be, until someone puts the poet in *Life* magazine. That's probably what he's after."

.

They stopped once, in a market town, for supplies, and to lunch at a snack bar with a Formica-topped table, a uniformed waitress, and signs advertising Coca-Cola and Seven-Up propped against the pork pies and bottles of orangeade. The parking lot was full of motorbikes, and cars with camping gear strapped on top, trailers attached behind. The food was standard, the sandwiches wrapped in cellophane. Afterward they filled a basket with lettuce and tomatoes, cheese, bread and butter and eggs. Sophie was looking at greengages and hothouse peaches while Alec went into the wine shop next door to the greengrocer's, and came out flourishing a paper bag with a bottle of wine in it, which he unwrapped to show her.

"A loaf of bread, a jug of wine," he said. "What more do

we need on this extravagant picnic?" She could still be irritated by his occasional meanness. The wine was a cheap white burgundy. But he had never pretended to a cultivated taste in matters of food and drink, in fact sometimes seemed proud of not having one, as though the lack testified to a certain seriousness in his character, a preoccupation with what was really important in life, a proper ignoring of what was not. It was the more annoying because Clive was a connoisseur of wines, and sent back to the kitchen a cheese that did not meet with his approval, blamed the cook for a fallen soufflé, not his own tardy arrival at table. Some of this had become a part of Sophie too. Food, she thought, should be perfect of its kind, or else it was hardly worth eating. Part of the bread from the sandwiches was still sticking to the roof of her mouth. She dislodged it surreptitiously with her little finger, looking doubtfully down at the piece of cheddar in the basket. After she had paid for the fruit she went back to the grocer's shop to get the Stilton she had really wanted to buy in the first place.

.

And so, by degrees, they came to the shores of the lake. The light had been going rapidly for the last ten miles, and it was dusk when they arrived.

There were several other cars, a panel truck and an ambulance parked on the grassy verge of the lake, and a small knot of people watching the water. Alec drew in neatly behind one of the cars, and they got out and walked to the outskirts of the crowd. Two small boats, seemingly overloaded with passengers, floated almost motionless a little way out from the shore. Someone got up in one of the boats and brought in a long pole with a hook on the end. On the hook, a tangle of waterweed.

"A drowning?" said Alec.

"They'll never find her," said a man standing beside them. He wore a cap, a tweed cape, knocked the dottle out of his pipe against his boot.

"Who was it?" said Alec.

"Mrs. Crawford's girl," said the man. "Oh, Mr. Forbush. I didn't see it was you. How are you, sir? And your lady?" A weathered neck, ruddy face, a countryman's eyes, sharp and clear, just the smallest bit hesitant. "Mrs. Forbush? I haven't set eyes on you in I don't know how many years. A sad occasion." Sophie shook hands with him. Hard, horny, and warm.

"Which Mrs. Crawford?" said Alec. Turning to Sophie, he explained. "They're all called Crawford, up here."

"Mrs. Angus, it is," said the man. He sighed, sucked at his empty pipe. "The water's deep. They'll never find her. She's off in one of them deep holes. Or slid off the ledge, most likely."

"How did it happen?" said Alec. "Go and get my camera from the car, there's a good girl," he told Sophie.

Suicide, they were saying, when she got back, picking her way carefully in her high heels. She did it on purpose.

"Suicide?" said Sophie, shocked. "How do they know?" The men in the boats stood up, brought in their poles. The crowd held its collective breath. Another draggle of weed. "And whatever for?" It seemed impossible in this remote place. She let her eyes linger on the darkening hills that rushed swiftly down to the water. A girl who kept sheep on the fells, knitted guernseys for her little brothers in the winter.

Alec took the camera from her, took some pictures of the boats and the little crowd, the flashlight bulbs falling like gentle hail to the grass. She looked at him with something approaching hate.

"She was in trouble," said their companion. "A married man, though none of us knew it. And we all know what that came to. It's an old story. They should have kept her closer to home." He threw an edge of his cape over his shoulder.

Closer, thought Sophie, than the necessary closeness of these dark hills and that dark water? The light was almost gone now. Someone on one of the boats held a flashlight directed at the end of the pole.

"A married man," said Alec, seriously, surprised, shocked. "Who was it?" And Sophie could understand why he asked, looking about the crowd. What married man here could appeal to a lovely girl? She already knew her as lovely. Among all the caps and capes and wind-grained faces and briar pipes?

"The poet. The Hermit. He's gone, acourse. Up on the fells, somewhere." So the poet was married. Sophie, who had wanted to meet him, felt suddenly he couldn't have been much of a poet after all.

"I'm sorry about this, Donald," said Alec, putting his camera away, being efficient, snapping snaps and buckling buckles. "Some sort of a relative of yours, wasn't she?"

"A cousin. Ay."

"They're all cousins, up here," said Alec to Sophie, and added, sotto voce, "inbred." He turned to the man called Donald. "I really think we ought to be getting along," he said. "Let me know. You know. If they find her."

She followed him to the car, and they drove to the opposite

shore, and walked along a path through the trees to his own place, beautifully neat and clean, the fire laid, needing only a match to set it going.

The window over the kitchen sink looked over the lake. Obstinately, the men went on with their quest. Sophie unpacked the food, glancing often out of the window, and the first flames leaped from the fire. They ate untidily, almost silently, rattling forks and knives, exchanging dishes of cheese and salad but not speaking much, sitting on the rug before the fireplace. The wine was sour.

"We could go to bed early," he said. "I'll show you the upstairs in a minute. Where the sheets are." He glanced at the window. "Would you like me to draw the curtains?"

"No. No, they'd think us — unfeeling. Better leave them open."

In fact, when the search was abandoned for the night, and the boats were beached, she placed a lamp in the window, as though it might be of some comfort to that poor girl, floating gently down, slowly descending to the drowned church.

"I suppose," said Alec, "that we won't be able to swim, after all."

The Roof Garden

THEY HAD LIVED in the apartment for two years, and been happy there, and thought they were lucky to get it. Finding it, being able to afford it, and moving in had all been part of the wonderful scheme of coincidences that made up their short history together, a history they still liked to talk about, as though to print it in their own heads as indelibly as paragraphs in an encyclopedia.

"I almost didn't *go* to that party," Ellie would say. "Do you remember, I had some virus, I felt wretched. I was in bed when Hillary called. I hadn't eaten for two days."

"But you came," said John.

"I filled myself up with aspirin, and called Hillary back . . ."

"And there you were, when I walked in," said John.

"Sounds like a song title from some lousy early movie, doesn't it?" said Ellie.

"Sometimes, those things are true," said John.

The apartment was pretty, light and inviting, small rooms but with big windows, and a little roof garden off the kitchen. When they first moved in it was filthy, every corner of it, and

Ellie had scrubbed and scrubbed, while John, using the most inexpensive paint he could find, painted the walls and ceilings. After a while, the cracks and damp patches showed through much as before, but they pinned up posters and a couple of African masks, and placed a pole lamp in a strategic corner, so that it cast as much convenient shadow as it did light, and then you really didn't notice too much. If you looked out of the window at the street, there was still ugliness, trash cans and garbage, rickety fences in front of the houses across the street, made up of pieces of corrugated iron and old bedsteads; but the front room of the apartment was almost unbearably hot in summer anyway, and Ellie kept the Venetian blinds drawn all the time.

Now the rooms were practically empty, everything of their own packed and taken away, except for a crate of books accidentally left behind, and their suitcases, ranged neatly together near the door. They were leaving for Mombasa the next day.

Ellie looked about her, and saw the shabbiness of the place through the eyes of her two sisters, sitting uncomfortably together (though they disliked each other almost as much as they disliked her) on the battered sofa, which was, as Ellie now saw, a disgrace. Although neither she nor John had ever thought to complain about it. They had even made love on it sometimes, and Ellie used to curl up on it when she was nursing the baby, or reading, absently eating oranges — the whole fruit, seeds, pith and peel. She thought of the sofa as a sort of nest.

"I wish you could have seen the place before," she said. "We have some nice things. It makes a difference, your own things." Her sisters failed to respond. "We have a silver coffee service," Ellie said. "The Literature Department gave us that. And one of the professors gave us a little hand-carved Oriental table. I had the silver out on it, over in that corner." Her sisters' eyes followed her pointing finger, obediently but stonily. "Of course, it meant cleaning the silver about every other week, you know that, what it does to silver to be out in the open air. It tarnishes so quickly, it'd go completely black if you let it." She sighed. "I just hope everything gets there safely." She was tired, she'd been cleaning the apartment since early morning, so as not to leave it in the state in which she'd found it. And she didn't know what to talk to her sisters about. Domestic details seemed the safest, but nothing was, not really. Now they'd think she was being sarcastic, since neither of them had given her so much as a teaspoon when she married. "You can use this for an ashtray. I'm sorry," she told Lana, the oldest of the three of them, who was dropping ashes on the faded carpet that belonged to the landlady. "It's really a shame. We have some lovely ashtrays. Jade. One of the Chinese instructors gave them to us. Too pretty for ashtrays, really, but that's what he said they were for."

"Though it can't ever have been a convenient place to live," said Lana, accepting the top of a mayonnaise jar, and grinding out her cigarette in it, so fiercely it was obvious she was dismissing all that Ellie had brought up, the silver, the teak table, the jade bowls. "These old houses, cut up into apartments . . . Rats. Cockroaches. Ugh. I can never understand what anyone sees in them. Though I suppose you were lucky to get anything at all, at that."

"Well, there's the roof garden, you see," said Ellie. "That's what really decided us. It's so romantic. Though you're right in a way," she added humbly. "We were lucky to get anything."

"Romantic?" said Meg. She sounded so affronted that Ellie flushed.

"Convenient," she amended. "In the summer . . . Washington, well. It gets so hot. Even John . . . And with the baby, it's been wonderful to have a place where she could play. Safely, I mean." The children in the street below, covered with sores from impetigo, the drunks, lurching in broad daylight from one lamppost to the next. "Our own little backyard, sort of, without the trouble of mowing the lawn, and all that. And right *in* the city, and close to the school." She might have been trying to sell the place. When they moved in, the area they now called the roof garden was a mess of litter, old newspapers blown in the corners, dead leaves from someone else's linden and oak trees clogging the gutters and the drainpipe. A rickety hutch of some kind, where some former tenant had raised rabbits, or perhaps pigeons. It was all so different now.

"Well, give me air conditioning, every time," said Lana, and Meg nodded. "Wouldn't be without it," they said together, and as though they lived together, though in fact Lana and her husband lived out in Silver Spring, and Meg in an efficiency apartment in Arlington, just across the river.

"They told us to take an electric fan," said Ellie, suddenly amused. "It was on the list of things we would need. But we didn't get one. John just laughed. He says the climate's better there than here. Anyway, he says we could always pick up an old used one, in one of the markets." She paused for a moment, imagining those markets, full of light and color and shouting in strange, foreign tongues, the women wearing handsome headdresses of twisted cloth. She'd meant to mention John as little as possible, but she couldn't leave him out all the time. She longed for tomorrow, when they would be on their way, across oceans and continents, away from everything. But tomorrow would come, after this final hour with her sisters, neither of whom had ever, after their original outraged astonishment, acknowledged her marriage at all, or ever invited her again to either of their separate homes. Not that she'd have gone, even alone. A Negro, they'd said. You're out of your mind. What are you trying to prove? All that schooling's gone to your head. Or maybe you're on marijuana? Hey, is that it? Has he got you hooked, or something? Are you on dope? I always said, go to a secretarial school, get a decent job as soon as possible after high school. Now you see what's come of it. It's wicked, it's abandoned. (Certainly, by them.) Ellie had tried to make it sound more acceptable, feeling craven as she did so.

"He's not . . ." And paused. "He's an *African*," she explained. What had she meant by that first, unfinished sentence? *He's not* . . . ? "He's over here on a grant. Like a Fulbright Scholar, in reverse." Nothing helped. She'd never thought anything would. Nothing could explain to them what John was like, under that black skin.

"All I can say is, I think you've gone stark raving mad," said Lana, on the phone. "Here, Skip wants to talk to you. He's just as shocked as I am." So Ellie hung up. She didn't want to talk to Skip, then or ever.

"You've come to the wrong door this time, gal," said Meg, with satisfaction. And added lugubriously, "Mother would turn over in her grave."

But even after all that, after the silence that continued when the baby came (and she'd spent a happy hour in the hospital bed addressing all the little envelopes, slipping into them all the little cards, inscribed with her daughter's strange foreign name), Ellie had wanted this last hour with her sisters. Heavens, they might *die*, and never know how happy she was! She and John would never come back to the United States. John was honorable. His country had sent him here to learn certain techniques, and back home he would go to apply them.

"John won't be here," she said, on the phone. "Just me and the baby. And I do want you to see her." Both sisters said they would call her back, and, after conferring together (she understood), they agreed, reluctantly, to come for coffee on her last day. John went out, obediently. He knew she had those two creepy sisters, and had in any case to see about the forgotten crate of books. He said he would come back about six.

"I don't understand you," he said, but agreeably. "After the way they've — But hang a white cloth out of the window when it's safe for me to come back." He smiled the wide white smile she loved, and to please him and make it something funny she would drape a white towel over the window-sill, as soon as her sisters had gone.

Lana rose suddenly, flicking ash off her skirt.

"I'd better take a look at Stevie," she said, and went to the kitchen door. Out there on the roof garden, Stevie's whining complaint had been going on for a long time. Isn't she ever going to see to that child, Ellie wondered. "He hates to be by himself," said Lana, "but he's going to have to learn, someday." Stevie, a fat blond baby, sat strapped in a stroller, his mouth wide open with indignation and misery. A zwieback Lana had given him to keep him happy and occupied had disintegrated into a mess of brownish crumbs all over his tear-wet face. A brightly colored string of plastic beads lay beside the stroller.

"God, are kids ever messy," said Lana. She picked up the beads and put them down on the tray in front of Stevie, and wiped his face clean with a diaper tucked into the stroller behind him.

"Quite a jungle you've got out here," Meg observed, and then, perhaps thinking she had used an unfortunate word, "I mean, like a hothouse. The Botanical Gardens, sort of. Didn't you ever want to get rid of it all?"

"We planted it ourselves," said Ellie, of the boxes and pots and stands of healthily growing green things, some with flowers, some without, some with leaves streaked with white, dashed with crimson. "It's one thing we'll hate to leave behind." They had enjoyed the planting so much, and been amazed and pleased at the way things had taken hold, little sticks of plants now grown into giants, curving gladly way above their heads.

"Probably got prickly heat," said Lana, of Stevie.

"Poor baby," said Ellie. "But we're in the shade, this side, this time of day." Behind one of the large stone planters she could see her own child, wholly ignoring Stevie's crying and the presence of the grownups, crouched patiently over a series of mud pies she was making with a small measuring cup and a tiny red watering can from the dirt at the root of a giant creeper. Neither Meg nor Lana appeared to notice her at all, as though, like some small brown forest bird, she had vanished into the foliage.

"Why don't you bring him inside?" Ellie went on. "Maybe he needs to be changed." Though Lana had not brought with her, as mothers generally do when they go anywhere, any large plastic bag that might contain clean diapers, a different toy. "You can change him on the bed, if you like." Presumably a clean diaper lay, closely folded, next to cigarettes and lighter, in Lana's smart purse.

"That little stinker? No thanks," said Lana. Apparently satisfied that all was well with her son, she turned back into the living room, plumped down on the sofa, and lighted another cigarette. "If I tried to keep up with that, I'd be busy all day long. *And* all night." But the child's cries were really piteous. Perhaps Lana didn't want to bring him into the house, change him on that bed.

"More coffee?" They nodded, and Ellie put more water on the stove, an excuse really to be away from her sisters' eyes, both probingly hostile and indifferent. She glanced out of the door at her daughter, squatting quietly over her age-old handiwork. Had she ever lain roaring in a stroller, indignant at being left in a wet and uncomfortable diaper? Of course not, the little gem, the little jewel, she had been tended like a queen from the moment of her birth. Except for the time they'd taken her on a peace march, and once to see the grave of Robert Kennedy, and then she had cried and cried, and they'd decided, Ellie and John, not to take her anymore, to give up some of those things they wanted to do — some of which had brought them together in the first place — until the child was older, and could understand.

Sometimes Ellie wondered if Meg and Lana really were her sisters, if they weren't all orphans, picked up one at a time by somewhat undiscriminating parents. They were all so different. But there wasn't too much doubt about it. There were facial resemblances, to begin with. They were all three the daughters of their mother, and of the same father, a salesman who sometimes seemed overwhelmed by the femininity of his household, by look-alike dresses, by the hair curlers, housecoats lying over the backs of chairs, and Kotex boxes in the bathroom. Ellie had few memories of him, she was born so much later than her sisters, but she recalled her mother telling him he ought to see a psychiatrist, because he was always in a foul temper. He never did see a psychiatrist, so far as Ellie knew, but died suddenly in a hotel bedroom in Detroit, of a coronary attack. Mother worked for a while, and then married the man she worked for, and went out to California, leaving Ellie to be brought up by Lana and Meg. Ellie had hated every minute of her teen years, worked hard at school only in order to get away, and was surprised herself at the scholarships and awards she won, at the fact that it did become possible for her to get away, go to college, lead her own life. All the years of her sisters' crying, "Ellie, have you done your homework? Are you studying up there?" (standing at the bottom of the stairs), had brought a result entirely unwelcome to them. She heard them now, in the living room, talking in undertones.

"Don't you think there's a funny — well, an *odor?*" said

Meg. "Do you think they really do — you know? Have pot parties?" Ellie smiled to herself, watching the coffee, shrugged infinitesimally. She'd tried it. Who hadn't? But she hadn't liked it, didn't like the crowd. She wasn't really a hippie, even when wandering from one Georgetown bar to another, dressed in boots and jeans and an old sweater, strings of beads about her neck. She was looking for something else, and had found it in John. Meg and Lana, though, would always suspect the worst. Meg had never married, was an old-maid schoolteacher who played bridge in the evenings with other teachers, cronies rather than friends. She seemed to hate everything about her life: the students, the courses, the principal, the school board, and the decor of the teachers' lounge. The way in which she boasted about beating her fellow bridge players seemed to indicate that she hated them too.

Lana worked on the Hill, or had, until her late and surprising marriage to Skip. Skip was a one-legged veteran of the Korean war, and when Ellie first met him was dividing his time between Walter Reed Hospital and Lana's apartment. She had been shocked once, on visiting there, to find him in Lana's bed, wearing apparently only the top of his pajamas, since the pink stump of his thigh stuck obscenely out of the bedclothes. Lana was annoyed to see her, and muttered something about making breakfast, although it was past noon. Ellie would have followed her into the kitchen, but Lana called over her shoulder, "Hand Skip his leg, El. He can't get up, if you don't."

Skip grinned, while Ellie wondered why on earth, then, was it placed out of his reach? Rigidly disliking the task, she brought the leg, encased in a pair of trousers, and ending in a neat dark sock and well-shined shoe, to the bedside. Then she made for the door.

"You don't have to do that," said Skip. "I'm a real expert at this. Turn your back, if you want to. But you don't have to." Did he have feelings? Was she hurting them by turning away? She stood awkwardly, half-turned as a compromise, while he got himself into the straps and buckles, and his good leg into the empty one of the trousers, grinning all the time as though he understood her dilemma. When he sat on the edge of the bed, a whole man again, she went into the kitchen.

"You're not going to *marry* Skip, are you?" she asked Lana, who stood, tall, thin and efficient, over the stove, laying slices of bacon on crumpled paper toweling. They heard Skip whistling, and stumping his way to the bathroom, and the loud rushing of water. Lana gave her a look, but didn't answer immediately. She stared out of the kitchen window at a neighbor's laundry, a neat row of six pairs of men's underwear, some shirts, a flock of diapers.

"Why not?" she said, at length.

Soon after that bacon and egg breakfast, she did. Stevie came along quite a while later, after (and despite that odd, almost despairing glance at her neighbor's laundry) Lana's drinking innumerable bottles of gin, which someone had told her contained ergot; and a bad fall downstairs in which she broke her wrist. By then, Ellie had been married to John for a long time — or so they thought, in their own way of counting historic dates — and Kumari was almost walking.

"Fresh coffee?" she said, going into the living room, and pouring the hot water right out of the kettle (which went with the apartment) into the instant coffee in the three cracked mugs (which they had decided to leave behind). She apologized again for the state of the place.

"Better, anyway, than a thatched roof and a mud floor," said Meg. Ellie was immediately angry.

"I've *told* you," she said. "It isn't going to be like that. It's a city. A big, beautiful city, a port. On the Indian Ocean. Not a tribal village." Though even if it were, she thought silently, even if it were . . . I'd still go. The crate of books, stenciled already with John's name, and their destination, Mombasa, comforted her. The two older sisters shrugged.

"Ah. Over There," said Meg.

"With Them," said Lana. As though a city couldn't really be a city, unless it were in the United States.

"Have you ever thought," said Meg, "that you won't be any more welcome Over There than you are here?" It was something Ellie had thought of, often. John's father had two wives. There were twenty children. But John swore they would welcome her.

"There couldn't be more prejudice there than here," she said.

"I wouldn't say I was prejudiced," said Meg, offendedly. "All I say is, people have their certain place, and ought to stay in it."

"You're missing the point, El," said Lana, lighting yet another cigarette. The mayonnaise jar lid was full of butts, and ash spread all around on the rug. "Frankly, if you want my opinion, I'd say your attitude shows some prejudice against your own race. Over There, Ellie" (she was being kindly now), "they are much more primitive than us. They hate us mixing with them, even more than we hate it. I've heard of a white girl whose head got chopped off. They thought she was some sort of a sacrifice to their Earth Mother. Or Earth Father. A heathen god, anyway."

"Oh, don't be ridiculous," said Ellie.

"Just wait," said Meg. "When that husband of yours walks into his mud hut, with a white wife and a burnt-toast-colored child . . . Oh boy." So she *had* seen the child, Kumari, half-hidden among the leaves.

"They won't hate me," said Ellie. "I just know they won't. And how could they hate the baby?" Twenty uncles and aunts, dozens of cousins! They couldn't all hate her. "They'll be proud of John."

"Proud? Why?" asked Lana. She couldn't answer for a moment. Proud? Why? She gave a half-laugh.

"You don't understand," she said. "We love each other. And we've got the baby. And I can cook . . ."

"In a earthenware pot?" said Meg.

"Oh, Meg!" sighed Ellie. "John says — "

"John says," repeated Meg scornfully. "Where *is* he, any-way?"

"I told you he wouldn't be here," said Ellie. "I told him to stay away for a while, so we could talk. He had things to do, anyway. We're leaving tomorrow, after all." Less than twenty-four hours from now. She wanted so much to go, to be on her way, she felt like weeping, like running out to the roof garden and snatching her little girl up into her arms, and leaving, *now*. Suddenly, she became aware that Stevie's crying had ceased. The same impulse moved them all, and they went to the kitchen door. There, in the shade of the green-leafed plants and vast tropical ferns, Ellie's tiny brown daughter pushed, with staggering effort, the stroller in which Stevie lay. Back and forth, back and forth. Contented at last, the fat fair baby lolled, chewing on a scrap of zwieback he'd found on the front of his bib.

"Hey, isn't that cute?" said Lana, smiling for the first time in the whole long afternoon.

"Well, at least they're keeping each other quiet," said Meg sourly. They were startled and amazed when Ellie, after watching for a moment, rushed out into the roof garden, and tore her daughter's hands from the stroller, smacked her angrily across her thin, toast-colored legs.

"Don't you ever do that again," she said, in a low, intense voice. "You hear me?" Another smack. "Don't you *ever* do that again!"

The others retreated into the living room, while Kumari cried, and Ellie went into the bathroom. When she came out, eyes a little red, she was walking differently, somehow more upright, and carrying a white towel.

"I think you two had better leave now," she said, pleasantly enough. She went to the front windows, and pulled the cords of the Venetian blinds. Sunlight sprang into the room like a tiger, lay along the walls, savagely barred. Ellie hung the towel over the windowsill.